Ca

Killer

A Freshly Baked Cozy Mystery

by

Kathleen Suzette

Books by Kathleen Suzette:

A Rainey Daye Cozy Mystery Series

Pumpkin Spice Donuts and a Murder
A Rainey Daye Cozy Mystery, book 14
A Pumpkin Hollow Mystery Series
Candy Coated Murder
A Pumpkin Hollow Mystery, book 1
Murderously Sweet
A Pumpkin Hollow Mystery, book 2
Chocolate Covered Murder
A Pumpkin Hollow Mystery, book 3
Death and Sweets
A Pumpkin Hollow Mystery, book 4
Sugared Demise
A Pumpkin Hollow Mystery, book 5
Confectionately Dead
A Pumpkin Hollow Mystery, book 6
Hard Candy and a Killer
A Pumpkin Hollow Mystery, book 7
Candy Kisses and a Killer
A Pumpkin Hollow Mystery, book 8
Terminal Taffy
A Pumpkin Hollow Mystery, book 9
Fudgy Fatality
A Pumpkin Hollow Mystery, book 10
Truffled Murder
A Pumpkin Hollow Mystery, book 11
Caramel Murder
A Pumpkin Hollow Mystery, book 12
Peppermint Fudge Killer
A Pumpkin Hollow Mystery, book 13

Chocolate Heart Killer
A Pumpkin Hollow Mystery, book 14
Strawberry Creams and Death
A Pumpkin Hollow Mystery, book 15
Pumpkin Spice Lies
A Pumpkin Hollow Mystery, book 16

A Freshly Baked Cozy Mystery Series

Apple Pie A La Murder,
A Freshly Baked Cozy Mystery, Book 1
Trick or Treat and Murder,
A Freshly Baked Cozy Mystery, Book 2
Thankfully Dead
A Freshly Baked Cozy Mystery, Book 3
Candy Cane Killer
A Freshly Baked Cozy Mystery, Book 4
Ice Cold Murder
A Freshly Baked Cozy Mystery, Book 5
Love is Murder
A Freshly Baked Cozy Mystery, Book 6
Strawberry Surprise Killer
A Freshly Baked Cozy Mystery, Book 7
Plum Dead
A Freshly Baked Cozy Mystery, book 8
Red, White, and Blue Murder
A Freshly Baked Cozy Mystery, book 9
Mummy Pie Murder
A Freshly Baked Cozy Mystery, book 10

A Gracie Williams Mystery Series

Pushing Up Daisies in Arizona,

A Gracie Williams Mystery, Book 1
Kicked the Bucket in Arizona,
A Gracie Williams Mystery, Book 2

A Home Economics Mystery Series

Appliqued to Death
A Home Economics Mystery, book 1

Table of Contents

Chapter One

I SIGHED WHEN WE TURNED onto Montrose Street. I was home. My Mama and Daddy had bought the house I grew up in during the first year of their marriage, nearly fifty years ago. Daddy had passed away almost twenty years earlier, but Mama would stay put in that house for the rest of her life, I was sure. The house had all the charm you would expect in an old Southern home.

A white picket fence surrounded the property, and the cottage style house boasted gingerbread trim and a wide wraparound porch. Magnolia trees shaded the front yard and rose bushes lined the white picket fence.

There was a large backyard with peach, apple, plum, and pear trees. The porch was my favorite part of the house. It was wide and accommodating, and Daddy had installed wide paddled ceiling fans so the summers would be more bearable during the evenings. Tears sprang to my eyes as we pulled into the driveway.

"We're home, kids," I said and wiped my eyes with a tissue.

"What a beautiful house," Alec remarked.

"Isn't it?" I said and opened the door to the minivan we had rented at the airport in Mobile. Mama hated to drive far, even though she was only in her early seventies, and I had decided it would just make things easier all the way around if we rented the van.

That way we would also have it to run around town if we wanted to.

The front door swung open, and Mama came out and stood on the porch and waved. I broke into a run and threw myself into her arms and started crying all over again.

How was it I had managed to move so far away and stayed away all these years? Moments like this made me so homesick I thought I would curl into a ball and never stop crying.

"What are you crying about?" Mama murmured into my hair.

"I miss you so much. You need to move to Maine so you'll be closer," I said. It was pointless to say it. Mama was an Alabama girl and an Alabama girl she would stay. I wondered how hard it would be to get Alec to move to Alabama.

"Grandma!" Jennifer said and elbowed me out of the way so she could hug Mama.

I took a step back and turned toward Alec and smiled. He had the back of the minivan open and was getting the luggage out. I went to him as Thad hugged Mama and introduced his new girlfriend, Sarah.

"Hey, I have someone for you to meet," I said.

He smiled at me and took my hand as we headed back for the front porch. Mama had my brother Jake put up clear Christmas lights around the edge of the roof and the porch railing. It was after seven in the evening and dark out, but the house was lit up so that it was a beautiful sight. A larger than life wreath hung on the front door. The wreath was decorated with red glass ball ornaments and red felt Santas.

"Mama, this is Alec," I said.

"Well, pleased to meet you, young man," she said and pushed past his outstretched hand.

"Oh," he said in surprise as she hugged him tightly.

"Pleased to meet you, Mrs. Hamilton."

"Now, don't you call me Mrs. Hamilton. That's far too formal. Allie has told me all about you, and I feel like I know you already. You can call me Mama," she said, taking a step back to look him over. Then she turned to me. "He is a looker, Allie. I must say you do know how to pick 'em."

"Yes, I do!" I agreed and laughed.

Alec went pink beneath the Christmas lights and glanced at me, looking uncomfortable.

"Well, I think I'll get the luggage out," he said and wandered off.

I looked at Mama, and we laughed as he retreated to the van.

Poor Alec. We Southern women were going to get the best of him.

"Let's get inside. It's getting late, and I've made a light supper for y'all," she said and led the way into the house, still chuckling at Alec's embarrassment.

"I'll help Alec with the luggage," Thad said and headed to the van.

Inside, the house was warm and cozy and smelled of roasted ham and sweet potatoes. Mama may have said she had made a light supper, but what that really meant was a small feast. She was incapable of making small amounts of food if she was going to be feeding more than herself.

"Oh, that tree smells wonderful," Sarah said and went over to the large blue spruce standing in the corner. She reached out a hand to touch one of its branches and exclaimed, "It's real!"

"Oh, yes ma'am," Mama said. "I don't believe in plastic Christmas trees. There's no real Christmas spirit in those fake ones."

Each branch was lightly flocked and filled with lights and ornaments. Tiny plastic toys made in the 1950s sat next to delicate German glass balls with glitter and painted scenes on them from the 1940s. Mama had draped long strands of silver tinsel on each branch, giving the tree a shimmering effect. I remembered being given that job as a young girl and being told over and over, to hang one strand at a time on the branches. If it had been up to me, I would have tossed handfuls of the stuff onto the branches and been done with it. Mama wouldn't have it.

In front of each light, she had swirled white gossamer angel hair, giving the tree a dreamy look. I had never had the patience to decorate a tree as she did, but I had to admit, it was worth the time and trouble.

"Wow, I've never had a real tree before," Sarah said. She inhaled deeply. "It smells so fresh!"

"My goodness, child, you've never lived then," Mama said and winked at me. "That's the smell of Christmas."

"No, I haven't," Sarah agreed, looking at the tree wistfully.

"I'm starving, Grandma," Jennifer said, going to the kitchen.

"I smell biscuits."

"They'll be done in about two minutes," Mama said, and then turned to me. "Come on into the kitchen."

Mama cooked on an old fashioned stove from the 1940s. I had admired it all my life, with its extra oven and warming bins. I had seen restored stoves similar to hers on Pinterest and eBay and had drooled over a pink one for months. It wouldn't fit the décor of my kitchen, but how I longed for that stove. I thought it might be worth a kitchen remodel to have it.

I heard Alec and Thad stomp up the porch steps and come into the living room. "I'll show you where to put them," I heard Thad say, and they went down the hall.

"So, how serious are you about that man?" Mama leaned toward me and whispered.

I glanced at Jennifer. She had finally settled into the idea of me dating again, but she still wasn't thrilled about it. She had finally admitted she couldn't argue that I hadn't waited long enough after her father had died. Eight years was long enough. But I didn't think she was ready to think about Alec and I doing anything more than dating.

I nodded toward Jennifer, who was checking out the contents of Mama's refrigerator and not paying attention to our conversation.

"Oh," Mama mouthed and smiled real big. "Well, I suggest that everyone get washed up, and we'll get this food on the table."

"Wow, it smells good in here," Alec said, following Thad into the kitchen. "Is there anything I can do to help?"

"You can set yourself down at the table, and Allie and I will have the food set out right quick," Mama said, opening the oven door and pulling out a pan of biscuits.

Alec smiled at me and did as he was told. We had all eaten very sparsely on the plane, and we were starving. There was nothing like home cooking, especially when it was my Mama's home and her cooking.

Mama put the biscuits in a red glass mixing bowl and covered them with a white flour sack dishcloth. I got the ham out and set it on the table, followed by sweet potatoes, green beans, coleslaw, potato salad, strawberry jam, and real butter. It was a feast, and I was going to have to do some serious running if I expected to not gain weight while we were here.

Mama bowed her head and said Grace and we started passing bowls and serving trays.

"I'm so glad y'all were able to come for Christmas. I can hardly believe I get you for two weeks," Mama said.

"We have so been looking forward to this trip," I said, cutting into a slice of ham. She had put cherry jam on the ham as it cooked, and it had caramelized and thickened into a delectable coating.

"This is perfection," I said after taking a bite.

"So, Grandma, how is the Christmas baking going?" Jennifer asked innocently.

"Now, don't you tease me, young lady. You know how it's going. It isn't. However, your Aunt Shelby brought by a banana cream pie for dessert tonight. She was in town this morning. But smart-alecky girls don't get any," she said, buttering a biscuit.

Jennifer snickered. "I don't know of any smart-alecky girls around here, Grandma."

"I can't wait to see Shelby and Jake," I said. I turned to Alec. "You'll love them. They're just like me, only not as good looking." I grinned.

"I have no doubts about that. You do look a good deal like your mother," he said.

"Yes, I do," I agreed. "Everyone has always said that." My mother hadn't aged much in the past twenty years, and I envied that and hoped I would take after her in that regard. Her hair was naturally curly, and she kept it short. The red in it had faded, but it was a pretty color, nonetheless.

"So, what do you kids want to do tomorrow?" Mama asked, looking around the table.

"Sleep in," Thad said. "Please. We flew to Maine in the middle of the night and then got on another plane early this morning."

"Sleep it is," she said. Then she turned to me. "I think we should bake some gingerbread men sometime this week."

"We" meant me, and that was fine. She could handle the decorating duties, and I would bake.

Gingerbread men were a tradition in our family. We used an old recipe called Joe Froggers. Christmas wouldn't be Christmas without Joe Froggers.

When I was a little girl, my grandmama had told me that Joe Froggers were a Southern specialty. When I moved to Maine, I discovered they were actually a Northern specialty, and I hadn't had the heart to tell her. I discovered that a man called Old Black Joe and His wife Aunt Crease had come up with the cookie, using rum to help preserve them in the 1800s in Massachusetts.

They were made into cookies the size of lily pads and were the best gingerbread-type cookie I have ever tasted.

They became the Hamilton family traditional gingerbread cookie, and I couldn't wait to make them.

Chapter Two

ALEC AND I WENT FOR a run as soon as the sun was up the next morning. It was nice being able to run outside again. The temperature in Maine had dropped to frigid levels, and we had given it up for the winter. It was cold here in Alabama with some frost on the ground, but once we got going, we warmed up nicely. I had my thermal wear on along with a knit cap and was feeling toasty warm.

"It's beautiful country here," Alec commented as we ran.

"Isn't it though? I remember running barefoot through the woods as a girl, and taking time to notice all the wildlife."

"Barefoot?" Alec questioned. "That sounds painful."

I shrugged. "Sure, I guess it was sometimes. But it was summer, and I always went barefoot during the summer. My feet were pretty tough. I guess it was kind of dangerous, but I was twelve and fearless back then."

"Fearless back then? What about now?" he asked, looking at me sideways.

I frowned, thinking about it. I had been through too much heartache in life to be fearless anymore. I was aware of more things that could devastate a life in the blink of an eye, like the accident that took my husband's life. And I was still having flashbacks from being shot at twice last month. No, I wasn't fearless anymore. These days I was working on not living in fear.

"I don't think so," I finally said.

"That's okay. One day you'll be fearless again," he said.

He said it with such confidence, I almost believed him. Could I ever really be fearless again?

We slowed down as we got to my Mama's house and then walked around the yard to cool down. We had been gone for an hour, and we had run at a good pace. I was pleased with the progress I was making in my marathon training. I sometimes wondered if I could ever really run an entire 26.2, but I wanted to at least give it a try.

Mama had ham and eggs frying when we got into the house. I could smell buttermilk biscuits baking above the smells of the other food cooking. It all made me feel nostalgic for my childhood home and my hometown.

"Wow, that smells good," Alec said, inhaling deeply.

"You've got to have a good appetite if you're going to hang around here," Mama told him. She was standing in front of the stove with a spatula in hand, and a yellow-flowered apron tied around her waist.

"Well, I'm in luck then. I've just worked one up," he said, pouring himself a cup of coffee.

"JENNIFER, WOULD YOU take this bowl of chicken and dumplings over to Mr. Turner next door?" Mama said to Jennifer, holding out a covered Pyrex dish to her.

We had just finished up our lunch of chicken and dumplings, and I had made an apple cobbler for dessert. Tom Turner had lived next door since I was in my teens. His wife, Jane, had died after breaking her hip and ribs from a fall down the porch steps. She had gone into convalescent care, and although it was supposed to be temporary, she had passed away while there.

I knew Mama felt bad for him, being alone and all, and she would take food over to him regularly. As long as Mama was living next door, Tom would never starve.

I sighed with contentment. I had eaten far more than I had intended, and I warned myself not to eat like this every day or I was going to have some post-holiday weight to lose. Mama somehow never put on a pound and was the same size as she had been in her early twenties. I must have taken after my father's side of the family, because even with running, I had to watch how much I ate, or I was going to have to run some extra miles to work off the food.

I helped clear the table as Jennifer left on her errand. Mama still washed dishes by hand, so I set the dishes in the stoppered kitchen sink and turned on the faucet.

"Need help?" Alec asked, bringing in three dirty glasses.

"Sure, I'll wash if you dry," I said, handing him a clean dishtowel from the drawer where Mama kept them.

"Oh, Alec, you don't need to do that," Mama said as she brought more dirty dishes in from the dining room table.

"Nonsense, I have some mean dish drying skills. Just watch," he said with a grin.

"Well—" Mama began but stopped when we heard shrill screaming coming from next door.

Alec and I stared at each other wide-eyed for a moment, and then he was out the door on the run.

"It's Jennifer," I said, shutting off the faucet and running after him.

Alec hit the front door, and it swung violently on its hinges. I hoped he had his gun on him, and then I saw him reach for it under his shirt. Jennifer kept screaming, and everything felt like it was going in slow motion. I couldn't get there fast enough.

Alec was in Mr. Turner's yard in moments, with me on his heels.

Mr. Turner lay face down in the side yard, with the Pyrex bowl of chicken and dumplings smashed on the ground not far from him. Jennifer stood next to him, screaming.

Alec was on his knees, checking for a pulse. "Call 911," he ordered.

I reached in my pocket for my phone and pulled it out. "Stop screaming, Jennifer," I said. I dialed and waited for the phone to be answered while Jennifer continued screaming.

Thad and Sarah caught up to us, with Mama hurrying behind them.

"Thad, get Jennifer out of here," I said.

"What happened?" Mama asked, out of breath. "What happened to Tom?"

The dispatcher answered the phone, and I had to take a couple of steps away from all the commotion to be heard. "Please send an ambulance to 728 Montrose Street." I gave her the particulars that I knew, which weren't much.

Alec turned Tom over, and the front of his shirt was covered in blood. The sight of all the blood sent Jennifer into more hysterics. "There's no pulse, and we've got either a gunshot or knife wound," he said to me.

I relayed the information to the dispatcher and hung up. We hadn't heard a gunshot, but I had learned from Todd Spellman's murder that silencers were still very much in use where murder was concerned.

"Please, Thad, take your sister home," I repeated, trying not to become irritated. I looked up, and both he and Sarah were white-faced. After a moment, Thad took Jennifer by the hand, and the three of them went back to Mama's house.

I felt a wave of nausea come over me. Mama looked pale and swayed a little. "Mama, why don't you go back to the house, too," I said gently. "I'll stay with Tom and Alec." Mama had been fond of her neighbor, and I knew this would be hard on her.

I heard sirens in the distance. "You can go next door. I can handle this," Alec said, looking up at me.

"I'll stay with you," I said.

Mama's hand covered her mouth as she made her way back to her house. Poor thing. Daddy had passed quietly in his sleep from a heart attack. She had put on a happy face in front of people, but it had been a devastating loss for her after more than thirty years of marriage. But at least it hadn't been violent, like this.

Tom's right hand was clenched in a fist, and I leaned in closer to take a look. I blinked. In his hand was a broken candy cane. Another wave of nausea passed over me, and I held my breath, willing it to pass. I was getting tired of seeing dead bodies and blood.

Alec stood up, and we waited for the police. Within five minutes, three sheriff's deputies, and an ambulance arrived. Alec introduced himself to the first deputy to get out of a cruiser.

The EMT's hurried over to where Tom was laying and knelt beside him and began examining him.

"Well, Allie Hamilton," one officer said to me with a big smile. "How have you been? It's been a long time since I've seen you around these parts."

It took me a minute before I recognized Elmer Jones, and I had to suppress a shudder. We had briefly dated in our junior year of high school but had broken up because he wanted more than I was willing to give.

I gave him a brief smile. "Hello, Elmer."

"I didn't know you were back in town," he said amiably.

"Just visiting my mama for Christmas," I said, looking away. I had no desire to talk to him, and I wished he would just attend to Tom.

"Well, I hope to see a lot of you while you're here. Me and Amy got a divorce last year. Seems she wanted more freedom, or something like that. You never can tell with some women these days. Maybe I could persuade you to stay here in Goose Bay instead of going back North?"

He had a big grin on his face, and the absurdity of what he was saying was stunning. A man had just been murdered here.

"Oh, I don't think so," I said, trying not to roll my eyes at him. "My home is in Maine."

Elmer hadn't aged well. He was balding and had a bit of a beer belly. I couldn't blame Amy for needing her freedom. Elmer's personality alone had done it for me.

Alec looked at me quizzically from where he stood, talking to the other sheriff's deputy, and I shrugged.

"Well, what do we have here?" Elmer asked, finally kneeling down beside the body. He grunted and groaned, and his knees cracked as he got down, and I wondered if he would be able to stand back up.

"There's a lot of blood, so possibly a gunshot or knife wound," Alec said, having walked back over to us.

Elmer turned to Alec. "I think I can handle this," he said curtly.

"Oh, of course," Alec said and glanced at me, questioning.

"Deputy McGinty over there can take your statement," he said, nodding to a deputy.

"Hey, John McGinty!" I exclaimed. "I haven't seen you in ages."

"Hey, Allie," he said bashfully. I went over and hugged him, even though I could tell it made him uncomfortable.

"Alec, This is John McGinty. I went to high school with him, and John, this is my boyfriend, Alec Blanchard. Alec is a detective in Maine," I said, introducing them.

They shook hands, and I was relieved John was on the scene, and that we wouldn't have to deal with Elmer. John had been the class nerd and was shy beyond belief. I had always wondered why he chose a job in law enforcement since it would require him to have so much contact with people. He took us to the side, and we gave him our statement. We didn't have much to say since we didn't see much of anything.

"Why don't you come next door and talk to my daughter Jennifer? She's the one who found the body, but I have to warn you, she's pretty hysterical right now."

"I'll watch out for hysteria," he said, smiling.

We started toward Mama's house, but Alec stayed behind. I looked at him over my shoulder, questioning. He nodded at me, and I went on with John to the house. I hoped Alec didn't get into trouble with Elmer, but I knew Alec would make sure the investigation was done right.

Chapter Three

JENNIFER SAT ON THE sofa with Mama, both of them sobbing in each other's arms. It broke my heart to see them like that. Thad and Sarah sat on either side of them, patting their shoulders.

"Jennifer," I said gently. "Officer McGinty would like to ask you some questions."

Jennifer looked up at me, and then over to John. She wiped her eyes with the tissue she had in her hand, and said, "Yes?"

"Have a seat, John," I offered, motioning to a chair across from Jennifer.

"Can I get you anything to drink?" I asked him.

"No, thank you," he replied with a nod. "I'm fine."

He sat down and turned to Jennifer. "Jennifer, can you tell me what happened when you found the body?" he asked gently.

She nodded. "Yes. Grandma sent me over with some chicken and dumplings. I knocked on the front door, but no one answered. I remembered going to Mr. Turner's back door when he didn't answer the front door when I was a little girl, so I went around the side of the house. He was lying there, on his face. I called to him, but he didn't move. I touched the side of his neck, and it was cold. Then I noticed some blood on the grass next to him."

"What did you do then?" John asked.

She looked sheepish now. "I screamed. A lot."

John began scribbling in his notebook and then looked up. "Is there anything else?"

"Yes," she said. "There was a plate of gingerbread cookies and candy canes on the porch floor. Right next to the little table he has there with plants on it. I thought it was kind of weird because the plate was broken, and the cookies and candy canes were scattered like someone had either slammed the plate onto the porch or dropped it from high up. It looked like it hit the porch really hard."

"I see," he said, making more notes. "Anything else?"

"No," she said. "I don't remember anything else."

"Okay, Jennifer, I appreciate your help. If you think of anything, you'll call me, right? Anything at all."

"Yes," she answered, sniffing.

He got up from his chair and turned to me. "Here's my card. Give me a call if you can think of anything. I'm sure someone will get in touch with you shortly."

I took John's business card and walked him to the door.

"I'm sorry you all had to go through this on your visit," he said. "It's sure not pleasant."

"Thank you, John. It isn't the way we had planned on spending Christmas," I said as I walked him out the front door. "Oh, and John?"

He turned back toward me before walking down the porch steps. "Yes?"

"I'm sure Alec will help wherever he can, if you'd like."

"Thanks, Allie, I appreciate that. I'll have a talk with him, and I'll be seeing you around," he said.

I went back into the living room, and Jennifer was staring into space. She looked up at me. "This is horrible."

"I know, sweetie, I'm sorry you had to see that," I said.

Mama got to her feet. "I'll get you a glass of water, Jennifer." She motioned for me to follow her into the kitchen, and I followed her.

She closed the kitchen door behind us. "Allie, that part about the plate of gingerbread men sounds suspicious to me."

"Well, Mama, the whole thing is suspicious since Tom was murdered," I said, trying not to sound like I was being sarcastic.

"I know that, but I think that's a clue to Tom's murder."

"It very well could be. I'm sure Alec will check it out," I said and went to get a glass out of the cupboard.

"If I had to guess, I'd say it was Ida Crawford that did it," she said, coming to stand beside me as I filled the glass with water from the pitcher in the refrigerator.

"Oh? Why do you say that?" I asked.

I remembered Ida from when she worked at the phone company. Once a month I went with Mama to the companies that we made monthly payments to, and Ida took the money for the telephone bill. She had red curly hair that bordered on orange and wore too much makeup. Her lips stood out to me, being a little girl, they were bright red and glossy. Every time she saw me, she would remark that I had red hair just like her. When we left the phone company office, Mama would tell me not to pay her any mind because her red hair wasn't natural, and it wasn't as pretty as mine.

"Well, she probably wouldn't admit it, but she was sweet on Tom. I've seen her car parked out front a few times," she said, nodding her head knowingly. "She still wears too much makeup, and that orange hair of hers is even more garish now that she's getting up there in age. She's almost six years older than I am, you know."

"You don't say?" I said. If I didn't know any better, I'd say Mama was a bit jealous.

"Yes," she said, lost in thought.

"How often would you say she stopped by Tom's house?" I asked.

"Oh, at least a couple of times a month. Always bringing him something to eat. Mostly sweets because Tom did have quite a sweet tooth." She sighed sadly. "Poor Tom."

"It is a shame," I agreed. I took a good look at Mama. Had she been sweet on Tom? I never would have thought it, but if it was true, then she would be even more upset by his death. She was also at a disadvantage to Ida Crawford because she couldn't bake anything, other than her light and flaky biscuits. Then I remembered that Mama had called me back in the spring and asked me for my recipe for coconut cake. I tried to tell her it wouldn't do any good for me to give it to her, but she insisted. Mama had not inherited the baking gene from her mother.

"I hope he didn't suffer," she said, and her eyes welled up with tears.

"I hope not. I think if he hadn't died rather quickly, he would have yelled, and we would have heard him," I said, hoping to make her feel better. I couldn't imagine there had been a struggle at all, or we would have heard something.

"Probably so," she said and wiped at her eyes with the back of her hand.

"Mama, were you sweet on Tom?" I asked. I figured I might as well be straight about it and find out.

"What?" she asked, blushing a little. "Me? No, not me. You wouldn't know it, but Tom was a ladies' man. He liked the ladies a little too much. If you ask me, bingo was nothing more than an excuse to flirt with the other women."

Mama sounded a little hurt when she said it. I wondered if he hadn't felt for her the way she did for him. Deny it though she might, she had feelings for him.

"But you liked him?" I asked gently.

"Now, Allison Marie, don't you go spreading rumors. People will be bound to think I had something to do with the murder," she said. "And I was right here, the whole time. And don't you look at me with that raised eyebrow. I'm not dead, you know. A woman sometimes enjoys a gentleman's company."

I smiled, but my heart was hurting for her. Whether or not Tom returned her admiration was unclear to me, but she had felt something for him, and now he was dead.

"All right, Mama. Maybe you can think of something that will help John and Alec figure out who killed Tom. He deserves to have his murder solved," I said and headed back to the living room with the glass of water for Jennifer.

Thad was peeking out the side window, watching the investigation. He turned when I came back into the room. "I'm going to see if Alec needs any help," he said.

"Stay out of the way," I told him as he left. "Here you go Jennifer, nice and cold. It will make you feel better," I said.

"Thanks, Mom," she said, taking it from me. "I just can't believe this happened. And why did I have to be the one to find him?"

"I know, I'm sorry, Jen," I said, and went to the window Thad had just vacated. The police officers, Alec, and Thad stood around the body, as the coroner looked Tom over. With Alec in my life, this was beginning to become a familiar scene for me, and I didn't like it one bit.

Chapter Four

MAMA AND JENNIFER HAD gone to lie down in their rooms, and I sat with Sarah in the living room, waiting. The girl was obsessed with the Christmas tree, examining every ornament on it, which was fine because it kept her from bothering me. Alec and Thad came back to the house when the coroner took Tom's body to the morgue.

"That was wild," Thad said as he walked into the house. "I've never seen a dead body before."

"You get used to it," Alec said. He gave me a lopsided smile when he saw me. "Your friend John seems like a reasonable fellow. But Elmer isn't quite so friendly."

"Yes well, you're not the first person who's said that," I said. "Why don't we go for a little walk? It's nice outside, and I could use some fresh air."

"Sure," he said.

I got up from the sofa, gave him a quick kiss, and took his hand. The afternoon sun was fading, and there was a slight nip in the air, but it wasn't terribly cold. I missed being able to go outside during the winter with just a coat on. In Maine, I had to bundle up with a big coat, gloves, earmuffs, and a scarf.

Alec closed the front gate behind us, and we headed past Tom's house. It looked sadly empty to me now, and I sighed. I could see the unlit Christmas tree peeking out from his front window. That made it even sadder. He put up that tree expecting to celebrate the holiday, and now he would never celebrate a holiday again.

As we got to the corner of his property, a brown 1983 Cadillac, looking like it was still in mint condition, pulled up to the front of Tom's house. Alec and I glanced at each other, then turned around and slowly walked past the car.

A woman with short, curly gray hair stepped out of the car, and I recognized Mrs. Beale, the county librarian. I had spent summers as a child at the library, reading as many books as I could so I could win the coveted gold plastic trophy in that year's reading contest. I had won six of them before I hit thirteen. Beat out twice by Sadie Beale. Yes, you guessed it. The librarian's daughter. I still swear she cheated and only skimmed the chapters. Everyone knew she wasn't a reader. Her mother probably gave her the cliff notes version of *Are You There, God? It's me, Margaret,* when she beat me in the sixth grade.

She didn't seem to see us walking toward her, as she made a beeline to Tom's front gate.

"Mrs. Beale?" I called out.

She stopped and turned toward me, giving me a vague look. Then recognition showed on her face. "Allie Hamilton!" she said, using my maiden name. "My goodness, how are you?"

"Oh, I'm fine," I said and went to her and hugged her. "It's been far too long."

"Are you here visiting for Christmas?" she asked, peering over her gold-rimmed wire-framed glasses, just like she had always done when talking to me at the library.

"Yes, I'm here with my family visiting Mama. And this is my friend, Alec," I said, introducing them.

Alec shook her hand, with Mrs. Beale looking him over. "He seems very nice," she said, turning to me.

"Mrs. Beale, Tom isn't home. Was he expecting you?" I asked. I didn't know how to break it to her that he was dead and saying he wasn't home just seemed nicer.

"Why yes, we play Uno on Thursday nights. I don't cook much myself, but he makes me supper, and we keep one another company." Her face lit up as she told us this.

Alec and I exchanged a look. I didn't want to be the one to have to tell her. Fortunately for me, Alec stepped up and handled it.

"I'm sorry to have to tell you this, Mrs. Beale," Alec began kindly. "But Tom passed away this afternoon. It was very unexpected."

"What?" Mrs. Beale asked, blinking. "What do you mean? I just spoke with him this morning."

"I'm sorry, Mrs. Beale. It's been a shock to all of us," I said, and reached out and squeezed her shoulder.

She stood and stared at us in disbelief for a few moments. I wanted to say more, but I couldn't think of anything.

Her face clouded over. "Are you certain?" she asked quietly.

I nodded. "Yes, we are. I'm so sorry."

"What did he die of?" she asked, and tears welled up in her eyes. "It's so sudden. I don't understand this. He was healthy. He went to the gym nearly every morning."

I glanced at Alec.

"All we really know right now is that he has passed. I'm very sorry for your loss. Do you know if Tom had family in town?" Alec asked. He used a practiced tone, and I had a glimpse into his life as the person that had broken this news to victims' loved ones far too many times in his life.

"Oh, yes. He had his daughter. She lives across town on Sylvia Street. But I'm afraid they were estranged. His daughter didn't like the fact that Tom... well, Tom," she said and trailed off.

"Go on," Alec gently encouraged.

"Tom dated sometimes. I never did ask him for details, but I heard his wife was in a nursing home for a short time, and he dated other women while she was in there. And Leslie, Leslie Warren is her name, couldn't abide by her father dating while her mother was still alive. I can't say as I blame her," she said sadly.

"I can see where that would be very difficult for family communication," I said, nodding.

"Oh, but Tom and I didn't date," she said, looking at me and shaking her head. "I mean, I didn't start coming over to play Uno cards with him until Jane had been gone for quite some time. And we've never really dated. I never did agree with Tom about seeing other women while his wife was still alive. If that's what happened, anyway."

"Oh, of course," I said. "I understand." Only I didn't. Why would she come over every week to spend time with him and not know something this important about him? Was he a cheater, or not?

"I'm, well, I'm just so shocked. This is shocking news," she said, looking at Tom's front door. "So unexpected."

"It really is. I'm so sorry," I said.

"Well, I suppose I'll be going now. This is all so shocking," she repeated. She looked so lost, I wanted to say something more, but I wasn't sure what. I hoped she had someone to share her grief with.

"I'm sorry," I said again, and I walked her around the side of her car and opened the door for her. She got behind the wheel, and I closed the door and stepped back. Alec and I watched the car pull away.

Alec gave me a sideways glance and then took hold of my hand and we continued walking.

"Well, that was something," he said. "Were you aware of his estrangement with his daughter?"

"No. And I also wasn't aware that he was seeing people while his wife was still alive. Seems kind of slimy. And don't you think it's odd that she wouldn't ask him for details about his love life? It sounds like she was spending a lot of time with him."

Alec shrugged. "She said they weren't dating."

"But don't you think they would have conversations? Wouldn't he mention the other women he had dated at some point?"

"You would think so," he said. "Sometimes people are odd though. Maybe because they weren't dating, she felt she didn't have a right to ask, and since she didn't ask, he didn't tell."

"I think she wanted to date him. Officially, I mean, and not just play Uno with him on Thursday nights. And Mama was always the one that brought food to Tom. Now Mrs. Beale is saying that he cooked for her?" Sounded to me like he was using my mother, and didn't really need her to cook for him.

"Maybe Tom just enjoyed your mother's cooking and never protested when she brought him food," Alec said.

"Oh! Do you think he recycled my mother's cooking?" I asked.

"Recycled her cooking? What do you mean?"

"You know. After my mother brought him food, he turned around and told Mrs. Beale that he had made it? What a cad!" I said, crossing my arms in front of myself.

Alec laughed. "You do have an imagination."

"Do you think Mrs. Beale had anything to do with the murder?" I asked, turning toward him.

"I don't think so. She seemed genuinely shocked," he said. "After being in this line of work for so many years, you get to where you can read a person fairly well."

"Did you see the plate of gingerbread men and candy canes on the porch when you were investigating?" I asked, remembering what Jennifer had said. "Jennifer felt like they had been thrown to the ground rather violently."

Alec nodded his head. "There did seem to be some emotion behind it. Maybe he insulted someone's baking?"

I looked at him, and he had a wicked grin on his face. "Well, if a person is stupid enough to insult a Southern woman's baking, then they pretty much have it coming. They shouldn't be surprised if they wind up dead."

He chuckled. "I could see that happening. I know a Southern woman that is mighty proud of her baking skills."

"I bet you do," I said.

"John sent the plate in to be examined. He was able to lift quite a few prints off of it. It may be a very important clue to solving the crime."

"Well, I hope so," I said. "What a shame. Killing someone this close to Christmas. It ruins the holiday for family members for years to come."

"I think it probably ruins quite a few things."

"Oh, and my mother thinks the killer is Ida Crawford. She used to be a cashier at the old phone company, back in the days when phones were attached to walls."

"Times have sure changed. No one has those dinosaur phones in their homes anymore. Oh. Wait. I'm sorry, but you have one of those dinosaurs in your kitchen, don't you?" he teased.

"All right, smarty. Yes, I do, but that doesn't make me a dinosaur as well," I said, doing my best to sound huffy, but not really meaning it.

"And why does your mother think Ida did it, besides the obvious fact that she worked for a now-defunct phone company?" he asked.

"Because she has garish orange hair and wears too much makeup. Oh, and she may have been seeing Tom on the side," I said.

He nodded. "Garish orange hair should be a giveaway. I'll have to ask John if he knows anything about her."

"That's a great idea," I agreed.

"Do you know Tom's daughter Leslie?" he asked.

"She's younger than I am. I remember her from school, but we ran with different crowds. I do remember hearing that she was a little on the wild side when she was still in junior high, dating more than one boy at once. That was frowned on back then, especially since she was only in seventh grade."

"I'm sure John will want to talk to her, as well."

A light breeze kicked up, and I felt a chill. I pulled my coat tightly around myself, and I wondered how many girlfriends Tom had had.

Chapter Five

I WAS UP EARLY THE next morning, baking fresh cinnamon rolls. There's just something about the smell of fresh yeasty sweet rolls on a cold winter morning that makes me feel nostalgic for my childhood and my grandmama. I had peeled and cooked up some Granny Smith apples with spices, raisins, and walnuts for the filling. Cream cheese frosting would top them off nicely. Decadent, but oh so good.

I was spreading the apple filling on my carefully rolled out dough when Mama came into the kitchen.

"Oh my, Allie. What have you gone and done?" she asked, rubbing one sleepy eye with the back of her hand.

"I am making the most delectable cinnamon rolls you will ever taste," I said, spreading out the filling. "If you make some coffee, these will be ready shortly."

"I can do that," she said and headed to the coffee pot. She put whole coffee beans into the grinder and turned it on. The kitchen filled with the smell of wonderful, fresh roasted coffee beans. She turned off the grinder and stood staring at it.

I glanced over my shoulder at her. "What's wrong, Mama?" I asked. I already knew the answer, but I wanted to hear it from her.

She sighed and then turned toward me. "Tom loved cinnamon rolls. I was just about to ask you to set some aside for him when they were done."

"I'm sorry," I said. "I bet Tom ate well with you living here next door. And I'm sure he appreciated it."

As long as I could remember, Mama was having me run next door with some of whatever she had made. Tom's wife Jane had been a decent cook, but she didn't enjoy it and tended to make simple and uncomplicated meals. Mama's meals were a treat for Tom. She loved to cook, and she loved to share it with others. She was one of the best cooks around. Just don't ask her to bake.

"That he did," she said and turned back to the coffee grinder to put the fresh grounds into the coffee pot.

"And I'm sure he appreciated all you did for him."

She nodded. "I believe he did. And I appreciated him. He sometimes cut my grass and trimmed my trees. Washed my car, too. Tom was a good man."

I smiled. Tom had been a good neighbor to my mother, and I was glad she had had him around to help her out.

The smell of baking cinnamon rolls wafted throughout the house, and in short order, people stumbled into the kitchen, still half asleep.

"There's coffee made," I said. Coffee was practically a requirement with freshly baked cinnamon rolls.

"YOU KNOW WHAT I HAVE half a mind to do?" I asked Alec as we cleaned up the kitchen after breakfast.

"No, what?" he asked, drying the pile of dishes in the drainer.

"Take these leftover cinnamon rolls to Leslie Warren. It'd be a shame if they went to waste sitting here. Cinnamon rolls are best when eaten fresh, after all," I said, pulling the stopper from the sink and letting the dishwater drain.

Alec frowned at me. "Now, Allie, we aren't in my jurisdiction now. You can't go sticking your nose in someone else's murder investigation."

"I don't intend to stick my nose anywhere. She's grieving and could use some support. If she just happens to give out any useful information, there isn't much I can do about that."

He snorted. "You could stay at home. That would prevent her from telling you anything."

"Now, Alec, that just isn't neighborly. Here in the South, we take care of our own. I'm going to wrap up these cinnamons rolls and get them ready to take over to her. You can stay or go, whatever you want to do."

"Now you're twisting my arm," he said, drying a cookie sheet.

"Wait. She knows about his death by now, right?" I asked.

"John said he was going straight over to her house yesterday when he left here," he said.

My cell phone was lying on the kitchen counter and chimed, letting me know I had a text. I picked it up to see who it was from.

"Oh, look, Lucy texted me," I said happily.

"Now don't tell me, she's going to come down here and help you run all over town and question people, right?" Alec asked, putting the cookie sheet in the bottom drawer of Mama's stove. "How does she know there's been a murder?"

"Now, Alec, that is a downright hateful attitude you have there. And after I made you homemade cinnamon rolls," I said, followed up by three well-timed tsk, tsk, tsks.

He chuckled to himself and went on drying the dishes. He was a good man, but he didn't understand how things worked in my world just yet.

So, anything new?

Not yet. We're going to go talk to his daughter today.

This stinks. I wish I was there to help you. I think I like being a detective.

I know it. I'm getting resistance from Alec. It would be easier if I had you to take along.

Let me know how it goes.

I certainly will.

I had called Lucy late the night before and filled her in on everything I knew, which wasn't much. Lucy had good ideas, and I wanted to run things by her to see what she thought. It really would have been easier to take her along to talk to people. I'd take Mama, but she was too close to the victim and it would upset her. Jennifer was a no-go as well since she was still shaken from finding the body.

Twenty minutes later, I had gotten Leslie's address from Mama, and we were on her front step. I had a foil-wrapped package of cinnamon rolls in my hand and Alec at my side.

The door opened, and Leslie stood there blinking, trying to place me.

"Good morning, Leslie. I don't know if you remember me, but I'm Allie McSwain, sorry, Allie Hamilton. From school?" I said brightly.

"Sort of," she said, her forehead wrinkled, still trying to place me.

"My mother is Myrna Hamilton. She was your father's neighbor. That's why we stopped by. This is Alec Blanchard, um, Detective Blanchard, and we wanted to stop by and express our condolences. And I brought by some homemade apple cinnamon rolls," I said.

She stood up straighter, glanced at Alec, and opened the door wider. Her house was in one of the poorest neighborhoods in Goose Bay, and it needed painting. It had been light blue at one time, but the paint had chipped and worn off, and gray wood showed beneath the peeling paint.

For a moment I thought she was going to turn us away. "Come on in," she said stiffly.

We followed her into the house. The smell of stale cigarettes hung in the air, and the room was sparsely furnished. I remembered Leslie being bright and cute when she was younger, but she had aged poorly. Her skin was sallow, and there were a lot of fine wrinkles around her mouth that reminded me of someone that had spent a good part of their lives as a smoker.

"Have a seat," she said, motioning toward an old couch that had large yellow and brown flowers on faux velvet fabric. The cotton stuffing poked out of it in places along the front edge seam where the cushions should have met the frame, but the cushions were so flat, they sat back a bit from the edge.

"Thank you," Alec said.

"I'm so sorry to hear about your father," I said. "I'm sure it was a terrible shock."

She sat on a dirty green overstuffed chair across from us, and rubbed her hands on her thighs, and looked around nervously. "Yeah, it was. I hadn't talked to him for a couple of years," she said, now looking at me.

"I'm sorry to hear that," I said, nodding understandingly.

"I remember you from gym class. You helped me when I couldn't do the rope climb. You held the bottom of the rope for me," she said, nodding her head.

"Oh?" I said. I couldn't remember the incident, and I had thought she was younger than I was.

"Yeah," she said looking away again. "I was in ninth grade, and you were a senior. None of the other senior girls would have ever helped me. But you did."

I smiled at her. "I'm glad to have been able to help you."

It appeared that Leslie had had a hard life, from the looks of the house and the neighborhood she lived in. Her hair was chin-length and tightly permed in a style that hadn't been popular since the late eighties. She gave me a smile, revealing a missing front tooth.

"Do you have someone to help you through this?" I asked. "I know it's a difficult time for you."

"Aw, sure. My old man. When he's around. Sometimes he's out of town on business. But it ain't much to me anyhow. My father didn't care for me, and I didn't care much for him. He abandoned my mother in that nursing home and went out and enjoyed himself," she said, her voice cracking on the last part.

"I'm sorry," I repeated. I wasn't sure what else to say. Leslie was in a tough life situation, and now her father had been murdered. Even though she said they weren't close, that didn't change the fact that her father was murdered.

"Do you know if anyone had anything against your father?" Alec asked gently. He had his notebook and pen at the ready.

She shrugged. "Any old woman in town, I suppose. He was a womanizer. I didn't know it when I was younger, but I sure knew it when Mama was put in the nursing home. He never went to visit her. Never. Just dropped her off and didn't look back. He said he had a life to live, and she wasn't holding him back no more."

Wow. I would never have suspected Tom could be so heartless. I glanced at Alec, who was scribbling in his book.

"Do you have any specific names?" he asked. "Of the women?"

She shrugged again. "Like I said, I hadn't talked to him in years. I wouldn't know anything about his personal life. He was already dead to me years ago."

Alec asked a few more questions, and then we left. Poor Leslie.

"Sounds like she had a rough life," Alec said when we were back in the minivan.

"I'll say. I would never have suspected Tom of being a womanizer," I said.

"Well, the thing is, she's grieving, whether she wants to admit it or not. People experience extreme emotions during the time right after someone has died, as I'm sure you know. But when a relationship is bad before the death of one party, the survivor either turns that person into a saint or a villain. It seems like it can go either way," he said, heading back to my Mother's house.

I sighed. "Yeah. I guess I know that. It does seem complicated," I said.

I was very glad that Mama hadn't gotten more involved with Tom than she had. This would have been heartbreaking for her.

Chapter Six

LATER THAT EVENING, I decided it was time to bake those Joe Froggers. Traditionally, they were made into lily pad sized and shaped cookies, but we always made them into gingerbread men, women, and houses. I hadn't made an actual gingerbread house since Jennifer was in the sixth grade. That was also the last Christmas we'd had with Thaddeus. I had intended to continue the tradition, but my heart was never in it after that.

Mama's stand mixer was from the 1970s and was struggling with the cookie dough. The motor was making whining sounds, so I stopped it and gave it a rest.

"You aren't going to burn up my mixer, are you?" she asked, leaning over the mixer to inspect it.

"Nope. At least, I don't think so. I'm giving it a rest and sparing its life as we speak," I said and opened a cabinet to look for a hand mixer. I finally found one that looked like it was from the 1960s. It was olive green with cream-colored swirls around the base. "Mama, I really think you should invest in mixers from this century."

"What for?" she asked. "These old ones worked just fine back in their day, and they'll work just fine now. Did cookie dough change so much that it's harder to mix in this century?"

I shook my head. "No, but age is taking its toll on them. Maybe you could get one and keep it under your cabinet and keep these more for looks. Or to mix something light and easy, like whipped cream."

She shrugged. "I suppose I could."

I smiled at her. "It's all right. They'll work."

I turned the stand mixer back on and pushed the dough down with a wooden spoon to help keep it moving and take some of the strain off of the motor.

"I'll get some bowls and put the decorator candies out," she said, turning toward the cupboard.

We had red and black licorice, round peppermint candies, M&Ms, tiny jawbreakers, and an assortment of other candies. I loved decorating Christmas cookies better than any others. There was something about the smell of Christmas spices that made me happy.

"Now, tell me. What did you find out when you went to visit Leslie?" she asked, opening up the bag of M&Ms.

I frowned. I wasn't sure how much to tell her. I wasn't sure she was aware of how Tom had treated his wife or not. "Well, we were only there a few minutes," I said. "Leslie appeared to have troubles with her father before he passed."

"I know," she said, pouring some of the M&Ms into a small Pyrex bowl. "Tom said she refused to speak to him. I expect it was because Tom was ashamed of her."

I turned toward her. "What do you mean? Why would he be ashamed of her?"

"Well, Leslie was one of those loose girls. She had lots of boyfriends early on. You remember that, don't you? And then she got into drugs, and Tom wouldn't allow her around his house for a while. Things kept going missing when she came to visit. She got her son taken away, too."

"What?" I said. "I didn't know she had a son. When did he get taken away?"

"About the time Leslie's mother went into the nursing home. That like to have killed Tom to have to do that, but it was only supposed to be temporary. She passed while she was in there though. Tom never forgave himself for it."

"And her son was taken because she was doing drugs?" I asked, shutting the mixer off again. "Did she get him back?"

She shook her head and opened the package of tiny jawbreakers. "No. Sadly, she never could get off the drugs. I'm not so sure she's off them now. I hope so, but I haven't seen her in a long time. Did you think she was on drugs when you talked to her?"

I thought about it. Leslie seemed to have lived a rough life, and it showed in her face and in the area she lived in. But she had seemed fine while we were there. A little spacey maybe, but I didn't think she was on drugs. "I don't think she was on anything while we were there. Alec would have noticed it, I'm sure. She was happy to get the cinnamon rolls. But it's sad that she lost her child." I couldn't imagine losing my kids. I doubted I could survive something like that.

"It is. I can't think of much that's sadder than that," she said.

"You know, she said Tom never went to see Jane when she was at the nursing home. Not one time. Do you know if that's true?"

"What? No! That isn't true. I wonder why she would say something like that? Tom went nearly every day, first thing in the morning. He loved Jane," she said, her face clouding over.

I was shocked. I thought she had been telling the truth. "There's a lot of hard feelings there. If Leslie was on drugs bad enough to have her son taken away, then she may not remember things accurately. I just think there's a lot of pain there."

"I agree. Some families seem to have more than their share of hurt."

It took some doing, but I finally got the dough mixed, and the cookies cut out and baked. Mama mixed up the buttercream frosting and covered the kitchen table with waxed paper to help with the clean up afterward. I lined up the cooled cookies on the wax paper, and Mama filled pastry bags with frosting. It was a real team effort, and I was glad I had her to help.

"All right, y'all, we're decorating gingerbread men and making a gingerbread house. Get in here, pronto!" I called.

It took a few minutes, but they sauntered into the kitchen, and stood, looking at the table.

"Well, don't just stand there looking," Mama admonished. "Have a seat and get to work!"

"Gee, Grandma, it's kind of late," Thad said, glancing at the clock on the wall.

"Nonsense," Mama said, taking a seat at the head of the table. "I know you college kids stay up until all hours of the night, doing heaven knows what. It's only 9:30. We have plenty of time to decorate."

"That's right," I chimed in. "This holiday only comes once a year, and you haven't been here for the last two. So, sit down and have fun like the rest of us."

"Wow, I've never made gingerbread men before," Sarah said, wide-eyed. She sat next to Mama, looking over everything set out on the table.

"What? Child, what kind of deprived upbringing have you had?" Mama asked.

"Apparently a bad one. My mother isn't big on baking," Sarah said. "How do we start?"

Alec sat beside me as Mama began teaching Sarah how to frost the cookies and decorate them. Mama wasn't much of a baker, but she had a steady hand and a good eye for decorating.

"So, gingerbread men?" Alec said.

"And women, and a house," I said. "Oh wait, don't tell me you've never decorated gingerbread men before?"

He smiled. "I have indeed had the privilege of doing so. It's just been about forty years since I've done it."

"Well, it's like riding a bicycle. You never forget," I said. "Here." I handed him a pastry bag and a gingerbread man.

Jennifer was already intently piping icing onto one of hers. She had been quiet all day, and I worried about her. She was a sensitive girl, and finding Tom like she did was hard on her.

I picked up one of the walls of the gingerbread house and began piping a thin curlicue line of white icing along the top that would join at the roof. I looked around the table at my family and I knew this was going to be a night that I remembered for the rest of my life.

Chapter Seven

"SO TELL ME ABOUT DEPUTY McGinty," Alec said as we drove over to the sheriff's station. I had a gift box lined with waxed paper and filled with gingerbread men in my lap. The smell of molasses filled the car.

"John? He's a nice guy. I went to school with him. He was always kind of quiet and shy. A nerd, really. He was a real math whiz as I recall. I thought for sure he would go to college and do something with that talent," I shrugged. "Then I heard he was a sheriff's deputy. Here in Goose Bay, they aren't fancy like we are in Sandy Harbor. They don't have any detectives."

He gave me a smirk. "Well, Sandy Harbor is about to be one less detective, come January."

"I bet you're looking forward to that," I said. I was looking forward to it, too. I had already said my goodbyes to my blog audience and had gotten lots of responses of disappointment, but understanding. There had also been lots of private messages, with email addresses and requests to stay in touch. I was going to miss it, but I knew it was good for me to move on.

I had written a blog on grief for eight years after my late husband had been killed by a drunk driver. I had grieved for my children and myself, and then, as time went on and I worked through it, I helped others through the process. Deciding to end the blog had been a hard decision. I had lain awake nights, thinking about it, and crying over it. These people were my friends. But going over and over the past can keep you tied to it. At some point, you need to figure out how to let go. And ending the blog seemed a reasonable choice.

Now, with Alec retiring from the Sandy Harbor police force, we would have more time to be together, as well as figure out what we wanted to be when we grew up. I was forty-five, and he was fifty-one, with thirty years of police service under his belt. It was time.

"Do you think you'll really become a private eye after you retire?" I asked.

"Well, it seems I have the experience for the job. There is another alternative, of course."

"Oh? What might that be? A blog?" I asked.

"That's certainly interesting, but I was thinking more along the line of sleeping in until noon and then spending the afternoon in front of the television, eating peanut butter Cap n' Crunch."

"I think that's going to get in the way of your marathon running career," I said.

"That's a possibility," he said, pulling into the sheriff's station parking lot.

I had a sudden flashback to my high school years as we walked into the station. My best friend, Cara Snelling, and I had never really been in trouble before, but we were brand new high schoolers, and we were feeling our oats. We had skipped school, hiding in an old abandoned house, eating a box of Twinkies we had bought on our way to school that morning. I had also bought a two-liter bottle of Pepsi, and in a moment's brash decision we decided we were cool enough to skip school.

One of the neighbors must have seen us through an open window of the abandoned house and called the sheriff. We were hauled off and threatened with trespassing and truancy. Our tears must have convinced the sheriff not to throw the book at us, and our parents were called instead. Trying to explain to my father why I had suddenly decided I was old enough to make decisions regarding my life was impossible, and I was grounded for a month and given hard labor digging a new septic trench in the backyard.

"Hi, John," I said when he opened the door to his office.

"Good morning, Allie. Alec. Come on in," John said with a nod.

John's office looked a lot like Alec's back home. A tiny desk that made anyone sitting in chairs on either side of it nearly sit up against the walls, and an old computer from the early 2000s.

"Wow, they don't believe in flat screens, do they?" I asked, looking his monitor over.

John chuckled. "No, not until old Bertha here kicks the bucket," he said, patting the monitor. "I'm afraid she's the last of her kind, and she's not going down without a fight."

"She's a beaut," Alec agreed.

"I brought you some gingerbread men," I said, handing him the box. "Joe Froggers."

He lit up. "My wife Cara loves those," he said. "Thank you."

"What? Cara Snelling?" I asked in surprise.

"Yeah. You didn't know? Cara and I married six months ago. Second marriages for both of us."

"That's wonderful. We lost track of each other after college. The last I heard from her, she had moved to Idaho with that wanna be hippie. He didn't believe in phones or much of anything modern, and I haven't heard from her since," I said in amazement.

He chuckled. "After fifteen years of using an outhouse and raising kids without plumbing or electricity, she left him. She finally realized that all he really wanted was to avoid having to work a job for the rest of his life. She moved back to town about a year and a half ago."

"Wow. You tell her I want to see her before I leave," I said.

"I'll do that."

"Have you heard anything new regarding Tom's murder?" Alec asked.

"Not a lot. Autopsy's back. We called in a favor, and it didn't take long. He was stabbed in the chest with a sharp object, but not a knife. The blade had a narrow point that widened at the shaft. Sort of triangular-shaped. Nothing back on any fingerprints yet."

"Any suspects?" Alec asked.

"Not really. We're talking to the other neighbors, but no one seems to know anything," he answered.

"Big surprise there," Alec said.

"I'd appreciate any assistance you can provide, Alec. It's nothing in a formal capacity, you understand. We've had a lot of budget cuts."

Alec nodded. "I understand, and I don't mind at all."

"What about his, um, lady friends?" I asked. "Mama and Anne Beale seem to be under the impression that Tom had some. Of course, that may be their imaginations at work."

Tom didn't seem the ladies man type. But I could be mistaken.

"We have a list of names given to us by Anne Beale. Women that he was supposedly seeing," he said. "But, I've got to say, I'm not completely sure it means anything."

"Why?" Alec asked.

"Well, he was seventy-five," he said slowly. "And there were more than a couple of names on the list."

"Like how many more than a couple?" I asked.

He smiled a little. "Like, almost thirty."

"What?" I exclaimed. "Are you serious?"

He nodded. "That I am."

Alec chuckled and leaned back in his chair. "Sometimes people surprise you."

"Can I see the list?" I asked sweetly. I wasn't sure he'd do it, but I figured I would know everyone, or nearly everyone, on it.

He looked from me to Alec and back to me.

"I don't know if that's a good idea," he said.

"She's trustworthy," Alec said. "And as much as I hate to admit it, she does tend to have good information on people." He looked at me, eyebrows raised.

I smiled smugly. "Yes, I do. I'm a people person, and I know people. Most of the time."

"Okay, but you have to keep this confidential, and you have to take into consideration that Anne Beale was shocked and grieving when she made the list. She also made notations next to each name. And grieving people tend to dramatize things. That's why I'm not sure this is helpful at all."

I sat up straight. "I understand."

He opened up the shallow drawer on the front of his desk and pulled out a lined sheet of legal paper, and laid it on the desk in front of me. The page was covered in small, neat handwriting. I picked the paper up and began reading.

Nellie Jones—sneaky and likes to drive around neighborhoods at night. Hmm, I didn't know that about Nellie.

Camilla Patterson—backstabber.

"Um, wait. Didn't Camilla Patterson pass away last August? Seems like my mother called and told me that," I said. Or was I confusing her with someone else?

John smiled and nodded. "Yes, she did. Apparently, Anne Beale might still be holding a grudge over whatever backstabbing Camilla did while still alive."

"Well, hopefully, Tom and Camilla are enjoying their privacy in the afterlife together," Alec said.

I went through the list, nodding at some when I agreed with the comments, and others I was surprised at. Then I saw it.

Myrna Hamilton—nosey neighbor and backbiter.

"What? Nosey neighbor? Backbiter? My mother is not nosey or a backbiter! How can she say that?" I said, feeling anger rise inside of me.

"Now, Allie, she put a dead woman on the list. How accurate do you think her notes are?" John said.

Alec was trying to suppress a smile. "Honey, this woman is clearly nuts. She put every woman she saw as a threat to her on the list and wrote whatever she could think of that made her angry in the past. This is the woman that said she never actually dated Tom. Sounds like she was angry about that."

I took a deep breath. He was right. They both were. "Well, if Anne ever darkens my mother's doorstep again, she better hope I'm not there to deal with her."

"Don't threaten someone in the presence of an officer," Alec chided, and then chuckled.

"I'm glad you think it's funny," I said. I turned to John. "Can we get a copy of this list? I know there probably isn't anything legitimate here, but you never know."

"Sure," he said and took the paper to make a copy.

"You think you're so funny," I said and slapped his knee.

John was back before he could answer me and handed me a copy. "Remember, this is confidential."

"Of course, I understand," I said, folding up the paper.

"We'll let you get back to work, John," Alec said. "And like I said before, if you need any help, I'm available."

"I appreciate that," John said. "I may take you up on that offer."

I read over the list again as we headed for the minivan. One of these little old ladies was a murderer. I was sure of it.

Chapter Eight

I WASN'T HAPPY ABOUT Anne Beale saying my Mama was a backbiter. How could she have ever said such a thing? I could remember running into her at the grocery store when I was with Mama, and Anne would run up and hug her and act like she was Mama's best friend. Some friend. I didn't have the heart to tell Mama, and she was better off not knowing.

"So did you find out anything new about Tom's murder?" Mama asked as soon as we entered the house. She stood twisting a dishtowel in her hands, worry creasing her brow, and it nearly broke my heart.

"Only that he was stabbed," Alec said. "They're still waiting for fingerprint results from the broken plate they picked up off his porch."

"Oh dear," Mama said. "That means a killer is still at large."

I smiled at her police-speak. "The sheriff's office is working real hard on it, Mama. I'm sure they'll figure it out soon."

"I hope so. I can't imagine who would do such a thing. Can you?" she asked, following me into the kitchen.

"No, I can't," I said.

But I have a list of nearly thirty little old ladies that might have. That was counting those that had already passed, of course.

I opened the refrigerator and pulled out a pitcher of sweet tea. It may have been December, but this was still the South, and sweet tea was always at hand.

"Well, it doesn't make any sense to me," she said, still wringing the dishtowel. "He was such a nice man. He would never hurt a soul. What do you think they'll do to whoever did do it? Once they find them, I mean?"

"Try them in a court of law," I said absently and poured a glass of tea. "Alec, would you like some sweet tea?" I called into the living room.

"No thank you," he answered. Northerners weren't much on sweet tea.

"But, what if it's one of his *lady friends*?" she asked, whispering the words 'lady friends' as if they were dirty words.

I looked at her. "Do you think it was one of his *lady friends*?" I whispered the last part as she had.

"I don't know. I don't know that he saw many other people in town besides his lady friends," she said.

"He was quite the Romeo, wasn't he?" I asked, turning around and leaning against the edge of the table.

Her eyes misted up. "Oh, yes he was," she said. "He was just very attentive, you know? He always seemed to know the right things to say."

I nodded. A man that had learned the art of listening could be the sexiest person on the face of the planet, even if he looked like a Poindexter. And Tom Turner was no Poindexter to the older lady set.

"Better than Daddy?" I asked, watching her.

She gave me a small smile. "There has never been anyone better than your father. On any count."

I smiled. Daddy would always be Mama's one true love. I picked up my sweet tea and took a sip. "If you were to say who might have done it, besides Ida Crawford. Who would it be?"

"Well, there's always Alice Woods. She was sitting with him regularly all summer long. Do you remember Alice Woods?"

"The lady that used to give me lollipops when we went to the bank?" I asked.

"Yes, that's her. Well, she has a temper. I heard her shouting at Tom late at night on many occasions," she said, nodding slowly.

"What was she shouting about?"

She shrugged and looked away. "I try to mind my own business."

"Mama, if you know something, you need to tell. It might help Alec and John figure out who the killer is," I said gently.

"Well," she said turning back toward me. "She wanted him to marry her, and he apparently didn't want to. They broke up in September, and I think she felt like she had been led on. I don't know how she could think he owed her anything, though. She had only been seeing him for three months. A Southern gentleman isn't going to be attracted to someone so forward." She said the last part in a confidential tone. Mama would forever be old-fashioned.

"Did you hear anything else?" I asked.

She shook her head. "No, not really. Oh, I need to get over there and water his elephant ears. I can't believe I've forgotten it these past few days. He would be so disappointed if he knew." She looked sorrowful in her misdeed.

"Elephant ears?" I asked.

She nodded. "That plant was special to him. His daughter gave it to him when they were still talking."

"Is it outside?" I asked. I had seen some plants on his front porch, and I wondered if one of those was it.

"Oh, no, it's in his kitchen. He took good care of it and didn't want to leave it outside where the sun might burn it."

"Wait. You have a key to Tom's house?"

She nodded. "Yes, of course. I always looked after his house when he went on trips. We were good neighbors to each other."

"Mama, why don't you give me that key, and I'll go take care of the elephant ears plant? Alec will come with me."

She looked at me doubtfully. "It'll die if it's overwatered."

"Alec and I will be careful," I promised.

She narrowed her eyes at me. "You want to snoop around, don't you?"

I gave her my most charming smile. "You know who I take after."

She narrowed her eyes at me, then went over to a small junk drawer in the cabinet that held the pots and pans and rooted around in it. I went and stood beside her and watched. She had matchbooks from the seventies, and what looked like hundreds of used and unused twist ties in there, as well as two sharpies, freezer tape, batteries, light bulbs, and an assortment of other small items.

Finally, she pulled out a worn brass-colored key. "Here it is. Don't you lose it," she said, handing it to me, but still holding on to the end of it.

"I promise," I said, and she let go of it.

I trotted into the living room where Alec was sitting with his feet up on the sofa, reading a novel on his e-reader.

"Guess what?" I asked excitedly.

He raised one eyebrow and turned to me.

"I have the key to Tom's house."

A smile spread across his face, and he put his e-reader down on the coffee table and jumped up. "What are we waiting for?"

We headed toward the front door, and he stopped suddenly. "Does your mother have surgical gloves? We don't want to contaminate the crime scene."

I turned and sprinted back to the kitchen, opened the cupboard under the sink, and searched around.

"What are you looking for?" Mama asked as she peeled potatoes.

I grabbed some gloves, held them up for Mama to see, and ran back to Alec. I held them out to him.

"Really?" he asked, looking at my offering of yellow Playtex dishwashing gloves.

"Take it or leave it," I said.

"Okay, if that's all we've got," he said, and we headed next door.

He put the yellow gloves on, and I followed suit. His gloves fit snugly against his larger hands, and mine were a little loose.

It was eerie, standing on Tom's porch as Alec unlocked the door. Inside, the house was dark and smelled stale, almost as if the house knew its owner was dead and wouldn't be coming back, and it had given up. I shut the door behind us.

Alec flipped the living room light on. It had been years since I had been in Tom's house, and I was surprised that this was no swinging senior bachelor's pad. Instead, it looked like a little old lady's house with frilly lampshades and crocheted doilies on the arms of the sofa and wing chairs. The coffee table was scuffed on the corners, and the couch was covered in clear plastic. The carpet was dark brown, and a vacuum cleaner stood by one wall, still plugged into the wall socket. It was a little old lady's paradise.

The sad little artificial Christmas tree stood on an end table in front of the front window. It's branches hung down as if it knew Tom wasn't coming back to turn its lights on. There were two stockings hung over the faux fireplace, and I wondered who the second stocking was for. Maybe it belonged to his deceased wife.

"Where do we look?" I asked.

"Anywhere. Put everything back where you got it. Make it look like we were never here," he said, heading over to a little table in the hall that held an old black rotary phone. He opened the little drawer on the table and started searching.

I went to the kitchen and saw the plant Mama had been worried about. It was drooping, so I turned the water on at the sink and held it under the stream. The kitchen was neat and clean, with dishes still in the drainer. I tried not to think about the fact that Tom was never coming back to put the dishes away.

I put the plant back on the plate that caught the draining water and began pulling open kitchen drawers. Utensils, knives, and serving spoons were in the first three. The fourth drawer was a junk drawer, very much like Mama's. I sorted through the various items, hoping to find something interesting. I sighed after I had moved everything aside. A brass key, like the one Mama had removed from her junk drawer, was in the back corner. I wondered if it was Mama's, and I slipped it into my pocket to try on her door. I didn't want anyone else coming over here and looking through things and getting the key to her house.

The rest of the cupboards and drawers yielded nothing out of the ordinary. It looked like Tom could probably cook, but nothing fancy. Things were kept neat and orderly, just as I expected.

I went back into the living room, and Alec was thumbing through a notebook. "What's that?" I whispered. Being in someone's house uninvited made me want to whisper, even if that someone was dead and couldn't protest.

"It looks like Tom really was quite the ladies' man," he said without looking up.

"What?" I asked, leaning over his shoulder.

"I found Tom's little black book," he said, looking up at me as I came around to look. "And it really is black." He held it up, showing me the front of the spiral-bound notebook.

"Wow," I said, trying to get a look at the names.

"Wait a minute. My Mama isn't in there, is she?" I asked, suddenly kind of freaked out. "Tell me she isn't."

"Hold on," he said and flipped to the letter H. "As a matter of fact, she is."

"What? Why would she be in there?" I asked.

"Maybe he couldn't remember her phone number, so he had to write it down," Alec suggested.

"Stop it," I said. "You don't think Tom dated my mother, do you?" Wouldn't she have told me if she had?

He shrugged. "I have no idea."

"I need to ask her about this. I mean, if he was seeing my mother, why would he be seeing other women?" I said, thinking out loud.

"Here's a thought, Allie. Maybe it's her business," he said looking at me.

I gasped. "Excuse me? Are you saying it's none of my business? Is that what you're saying?"

He shrugged and went back to looking through the book.

"Well, it is my business. She's my mother," I said.

"Okay," he said noncommittally.

I huffed and went into the bathroom to see if anything was in there. Alec had no idea what he was talking about. I needed to keep an eye on my mother, even if it was from a distance.

"It's just an address book, Allie," Alec called from the hall. "It's nothing to get excited about."

I sighed but didn't answer him.

Chapter Nine

I OPENED TOM'S MEDICINE cabinet and found the usual array of meds an older person might have. High blood pressure, high cholesterol, and another for acid reflux. I sighed. In spite of what we'd been told, including the list John had given us and the little black book Alec had found, it was still hard for me to see Tom Turner as someone anyone would want to kill.

I closed the medicine cabinet and opened the cupboard under the sink. I found the usual items there. Toilet paper, soap, cleaning supplies. I stood back up and wandered into the guest bedroom across the hall.

The room was done in dusky blues reminiscent of the country blue themes many Southern homes had featured back in the late eighties. A queen-size bed was positioned in the corner and covered in that dusky blue coverlet and blue sham-covered pillows. Three decorator pillows in the same blue and covered in cream-colored embroidered flowers sat in front of the bed pillows. Two square and one round.

I sat on the edge of the bed and pulled out the drawer in the bedside table. Huh. There was an empty prescription bottle with Mable Townsend's name on it. I tried to remember who Mabel was, but I drew a blank. I didn't recognize the drug, so I pulled my phone out of my pocket and Googled the name, fumbling with the buttons in my Playtex rubber gloves.

Well, whoever Mabel was, it looked like she had high blood pressure. I set it on the top of the bedside table and pulled out an old TV Guide from 1998 featuring Jerry Seinfeld on the cover. Next, I found a prayer card from the Catholic Church and an index card with a recipe for oatmeal cookies. I read it over, and it sounded good, so I borrowed it. Tom wasn't going to be baking cookies any time soon, anyway.

The closet was empty except for a couple of sweaters and ladies' cardigans. I wondered if Mabel had been a long time guest of Tom's. Or maybe she was a relative? The room was neat and tidy, and there wasn't much left to look at, so I went in search of Alec.

I found him rummaging through Tom's bedside table, setting each item on top of it.

"Look what I found," I said, holding up the medicine bottle. "Oh, and a recipe for oatmeal cookies. They sound good. I'll have to make some while we're here."

"Who's Mabel?" he asked, examining the label on the bottle.

I shrugged. "I don't know, but there are a couple of ladies' sweaters in the guest bedroom. My mother might know her."

"Well, the house seems pretty clean so far," he commented.

I sat on the edge of the bed and looked around the room. Tom kept a clean house. He didn't go in much for knick-knacks, and there were vacuum marks on the dark brown carpeting. There was another bedside table with a small lamp on it on the other side of the queen-size bed. A small glass and a small plate with crumbs sat on top of the table, pushed to the back corner. I got up and went around to the other side of the bed.

"This is one of my mother's plates," I said, picking it up. There was a dark smear covering the pink rose pattern on it and dark crumbs. I brought it to my nose and sniffed. "Chocolate."

"So maybe your mother brought him a snack?" Alec asked, not looking at me.

"My mother can't bake," I reminded him. "Why would it have chocolate on it? Cake or brownies, I'm guessing."

"Maybe she brought him something else, and then he used the plate for a chocolatey bedtime snack," he said, still rummaging through the drawer. There he went, being pragmatic again, and probably completely right. I hated when he was right.

"Maybe. But what would she have brought him on this small of a plate? My mother cooks, but she doesn't bake, and this is a dessert plate. I can't imagine what she might have brought him on such a small plate if it wasn't dessert."

Alec snickered. "Maybe she brought him one biscuit?"

"Yeah, right," I said. "My mother doesn't do one biscuit." I picked up the small glass, and it had a dried white ring on the inside bottom. Whatever he had eaten, he had had a glass of milk to go with it. What else would it be except cake or brownies? Or a frosted chocolate cookie? I added the plate to my medicine bottle find.

We went through the house, room by room, cupboard by cupboard. Nothing seemed out of the ordinary. Tom's house was small, but it did have a den. I stepped down into the darkened room and flipped on the light switch.

"Wow," I said. Tom was a collector of sorts. Swords and daggers were hanging on the walls. Some were mounted on wood, and some hung by wires on the wall. Most had intricate handle carvings, and some had curved blades. I couldn't tell if this stuff was genuine and expensive, or something you bought at Walmart. But at first glance, it looked impressive.

"Wow is right," Alec agreed, stepping down into the room. "Want to bet the murder weapon was hanging on the wall somewhere? John and I were rather surprised by this find."

"I think I know how that bet would land," I said. There were several places on the wall that were bare. In some places, there were nail holes in the wall, and some had thin wire hangers still attached to the wall.

We took a closer look at the daggers hanging on the wall. Alec picked up one that had a spiky edged patterned blade and held it close to examine it. "Getting stabbed with this thing would be vicious," he said. "When you pull it out, it would rip out some flesh."

I shuddered. "Thanks for the visual."

He put the dagger back. "John had some of the missing items taken to the lab, but there were some bare spots when we were here the day of the murder."

I nodded. "Do you know how many items John took? It looks like at least nine are missing."

"More than that. See that credenza? There are empty stands there. I'll ask John and see what he says."

"So, have we learned anything?" I asked as we looked around the room.

He shook his head. "Not much. I didn't get to look this thoroughly the day of the murder, so I'm glad your mother had the key. But, the notebook might come in handy. We'll ask your mother if she knows anything about the people listed in it. It might just be an address book. There are some men's names in it, including people with the same last name as his."

"Is Mabel in the notebook?" I asked.

He opened it up and flipped to T and then turned the page. He shook his head. "No. Mabel is not in here."

"That's odd," I said. "Maybe Mama knows who she is."

We searched the rest of the house, including the garage, and didn't find much else to go on. On our way out the front door, I stopped. There had been vacuum marks in the bedroom, and every other room that had carpet, including the living room. The carpet was old and had a longer nap than what was sold in stores today. The vacuum marks were clear because of the length of the nap. Except right in front of the La-Z-Boy, the carpet was pressed down.

"Hey," I said to Alec's back as he opened the front door. He turned to look at me. "Look at the carpet in front of the La-Z-Boy. It's flattened, and the flattened area extends in front of the sofa."

"He may have spent some time in front of the television before he died," he said.

"Maybe. But the vacuum is still plugged into the wall and sitting out. Everything in this house is neat and in order. Nothing is left out, except this plate and the milk glass. Other than that, it's neat," I said. "Maybe the killer came in the house, and they argued and then struggled in front of the sofa and chair, right before they killed him. He could have run outside to try to escape and collapsed."

"Good eye, Columbo. I'll make a note of it. John has already taken fingerprints, although if Tom's as much a ladies man as certain people seem to think, they're likely to find a few of them. We can use Luminol to see if there's any blood on the carpet."

"See? I'm a good investigator," I said.

"Of course you are," he said.

We walked out of the house, locking the door behind us. Alec had the little black book, and I had Mama's plate and Mabel's medicine bottle.

"Can we get in trouble for removing this stuff from Tom's house? Can you get in trouble for stealing from the dead?" I asked as we headed back to my mother's house.

"Yes, as a matter of fact, you can get in trouble for stealing from the dead, although usually it's called grave robbing. But obviously, we didn't rob from the grave. And removing evidence is a huge no-no. But we'll put it back when we're done with it," he said. "We don't want to spend Christmas in jail."

"No, an orange jumpsuit still won't go with my red hair," I said.

Chapter Ten

"MAMA," I CALLED AS we entered the house. "Mama?"

"Yes, dear?" she asked, poking her head out the kitchen door.

"I found something next door," I said, holding up the plate with the pink roses on it.

Her brow furrowed as she looked intently at the plate, but she didn't say anything.

"Well? It smells like chocolate," I said, holding the plate under my nose. "And since you don't bake, I'm wondering why?"

"Well, Allie, just because you know I can't bake, doesn't mean others think I can't bake." She gave me a big smile and walked into the living room and took a seat on the sofa.

"Ew, Mom, that's kind of gross. Stealing a dead man's plate and smelling it?" Thad said, not bothering to look up from his iPad.

"Whatever, Thad. Mama, did you take Tom a store-bought cake and tell him you baked it?" I was going to get to the bottom of this.

Mama breathed out deeply. "Allie, that's ridiculous. I would never do that."

"No?" I asked, not sure I believed her.

Alec sat next to Thad and pulled his phone out of his pocket. "I don't know what difference it makes," he said.

"Yes, what difference does it make?" Mama asked, feeling smug with Alec's support.

"All right, then. You can make dessert tonight," I said and headed toward the kitchen.

"Someone needs to be more respectful to their mother," Alec called to my back.

I hated when he was right. It didn't really matter, but I was nosey as could be, and I wanted to know. I put the plate in the sink and ran water over it.

"I don't know why you have to make a big deal over this," Mama hissed as she came up behind me.

I shrugged. "I told you before, you know who I take after." I gave her a big smile. I wasn't intending to be mean, I just wanted to know what was going on with her.

"All right. I bought brownies at the Piggly Wiggly, and I brought him one. And told him I made it. I had so much competition with the other ladies bringing him sweets and things. I had to fight back somehow," she admitted, turning pink.

"Mama, why did you think you had competition? You don't need to bribe a man with food to get him to like you. You're just about the best person in this town. You're caring, you help people all the time, you're sweet and you're smart," I said, turning toward her. "Any man should be lucky to have you. If that's what you really want."

She sighed and leaned against the kitchen counter. "I know I shouldn't have felt that way, but I just kept seeing Ida and Anne showing up there. I knew they were bringing him baked goods, and I couldn't do that unless I cheated. He never knew the difference."

"Well, I guess that just shows you he had no taste in women, nor dessert. He had someone as wonderful as you living right next door, and he was looking around," I said. "And if he had been a real foodie, he would have known those baked goods came from the grocery store."

"Unless he was just trying to be nice, I suppose," she said wistfully. "He really was a nice man, you know."

I ignored that. I was having doubts as to whether Tom Turner was a nice man or not.

"We have something to show you," I said. I went to the kitchen door and signaled to Alec to come into the kitchen.

He looked at me quizzically as he entered the kitchen.

"Where's that notebook?" I asked.

"Hold on," he said and went and got it from the living room.

"Mama, can you tell us how many of the names in this book are local women? I know some of them, but not all of them," I said, sitting at the kitchen table.

Mama sat next to me, and Alec sat across from me, and I opened the notebook.

"Oh, looks like an address book," she said. Her reading glasses hung from a chain around her neck, and she put them on. "Oh, Naomi Appleby. She's the checker at the Piggly Wiggly. Well, she used to be. She passed away last summer. I heard it was a heart attack."

"Oh, that's sad," I said. "How about Hattie Atkins?"

"Oh, Hattie runs bingo down at the Catholic church on Saturday nights," she said. "She's a nice lady."

"So, still alive?" I asked.

"Yes, quite," she said. "And Natalie Baker is still alive, too. She used to work as a secretary at the used car lot that was down on First Avenue. You remember her, don't you?"

I nodded, although I really didn't. It was amazing how you could forget so much of the town that you grew up in when you didn't visit often.

Alec was making notes in his own notebook as we talked. I wondered what he was thinking. We were going over an elderly man's little black book that was probably nothing more than an address book. It didn't seem useful.

"Oh, there's Janice Cates. That's an evil one, if you ask me," Mama said, nodding her head. "I wouldn't put it past her to kill Tom. She has a temper, that one does."

"Oh? Evil in what way?" I asked.

"She double charged me for my bananas at the Piggly Wiggly one time. I told her I wasn't going to let her do that to me, and she had the audacity to argue with me," she said, looking at me very seriously.

I sighed and glanced at Alec, who had stopped writing to look at her. I could tell by the incredulous look on his face that he was having trouble believing what she was saying.

"Mama, stop it. That doesn't make someone evil, and you know it," I said. "Let's move on."

"No, that just shows she was mean. Even when she knew he was wrong, she argued with me. But what made her evil is that Rita Smith's daughter, Hayley Sue, used to work at the Piggly Wiggly with Janice, and Janice didn't like Hayley Sue on account of Rita not liking Janice. Rita Smith is so sweet I can't imagine anyone not liking her. But Janice always gave Hayley Sue a hard time. She was the newest cashier, and it was her first job. Well, Hayley Sue had just gotten married, and a few months later she was pregnant, but her husband got laid off at the lumber yard because the price of houses had fallen, and they were depending on Hayley Sue's wages at the Piggly Wiggly."

"Mama, is there a point to this story?" I asked. I was worried she was just going to keep talking without ever getting there.

"Well, of course! She never was a patient child you know, Alec," she said, looking at him.

"Oh, you don't have to tell me that. I understand completely," he said, giving me the eye.

I rolled my eyes at him. I could be patient. Sometimes. I just chose not to be. Most of the time.

"As I was saying, before I was interrupted," Mama continued, nodding at me. "Janice told the manager that Hayley Sue was stealing money from her cash drawer. So the manager went, and surprise counted Hayley Sue's cash drawer, and it was short one hundred dollars." Mama had a smug look on her face as if she had just proven her point, but I couldn't see it.

"I don't understand. If Hayley Sue's cash drawer was short, then why is that Janice being evil?" I asked.

"Because Hayley Sue was newly pregnant and having morning sickness all day long. That day, Hayley Sue got real sick and had to rush to the bathroom, but she had a line of customers. Janice was passing by, just coming back off her lunch hour, and Hayley Sue asked Janice to take over her drawer for a minute, which she did. And then Janice went and told the manager what she told him, and the money was missing."

I looked at Alec.

"Yes, but that doesn't prove anything. What if Hayley Sue just made an honest mistake and miscounted? You know, because she wasn't feeling well?" he asked.

"I guess that could be, but how did Janice know to tell the manager that day?" Mama pointed out.

She did have a point there. "How do you know she was the one that told the manager?" I asked.

"She bragged about it. She said she had seen Hayley Sue pocket the money, but anyone that knows Hayley Sue knows it isn't true. She's the sweetest girl you ever met."

"Did you see Janice over at Tom's?" Alec asked.

Mama nodded solemnly. "Yes. Lots. She brought him dinner at least every other week. And I heard them arguing sometimes. Once, she was screaming at him that he didn't appreciate her, and he'd be sorry. And she slammed his screen door so hard I thought it would come off the hinges. She pulled away from the curb so fast, she left black skid marks in the street."

I tilted my head, looking at Alec as he scribbled in his notebook. "When was the last time you saw Janice over at Tom's?" he asked without looking up.

"Oh, I'd say it's been a few weeks. I don't know, but I thought they might have gotten in an argument again because she skipped bringing him dinner last Wednesday," she said.

"Who do you know, besides me, that bakes gingerbread men? I know it's Christmas, and it could be anyone, but is there someone that stands out to you?" I asked her.

"Yes, Charlotte Moody."

"I remember her. She was my friend Tammy's aunt," I said. I remembered Charlotte being a quiet woman of few words. Sometimes it seemed she didn't speak at all. She always smiled when she saw me, and since she didn't talk much, she never required much out of me.

I sat back and watched as Mama flipped through the notebook, and Alec took notes of the interesting ones. I was beginning to wonder if anything she said would lead us to the killer, or if these were just small-town stories being passed on. Someone had done the deed, and we needed to know who. I just wasn't sure we were going to find out anything from the people Mama was pointing out.

Chapter Eleven

ALEC AND I HAD DECIDED on dinner out. My sister was coming to visit in the morning, and I knew things would get hectic, so I wanted some alone time with Alec. We were at The Pitt. The Pitt was a barbecue place that featured the most tender brisket and steaks you could imagine. Not to mention beef ribs that fell off the bone. You could smell the smoking oak wood for a couple of miles around. It was one of my favorite places to eat when I came home to visit.

"So, what do you recommend?" Alec asked, looking over the menu.

"Mmm, anything. Everything is good here. But if you like to get messy, the ribs can't be beat," I said.

It was after six o'clock in the evening, and the place was filling up fast. The room was warm and felt good after being outside in the chilly air. The ambiance of The Pitt was warm and homey. Each booth and table was covered in a red and white check tablecloth, and cold drinks were served in Mason jars.

"I think I'm going to have to go with those ribs," Alec said after looking over the menu a few more minutes. "Now what about sides?"

"Well, you have to go with the coleslaw. It's famous all over the county. And the beans are wonderful, too. I'm going to have a side salad with ranch along with the beans, and I think I'll have the brisket."

The waitress came and set a basket of sliced garlic toast on the table and took our orders. "I'll be right back with your food," she said with a smile and was gone.

"Well, look who's here," Alec said, looking over my head.

I turned and looked behind me. Elmer Jones. It took all I had not to curl my lip in disgust. I turned back to Alec. "Maybe he won't see us."

"I don't think we're in luck there," he said.

Elmer was beside our table lightning quick.

"Hey, Allie, how you doing?" he said, ignoring Alec.

"I'm wonderful, Elmer. You've met my boyfriend, Alec, haven't you?" I said. I couldn't help myself. Nobody ignores Alec and gets away with it on my watch.

The smile left Elmer's face, but he didn't look at Alec. "Yeah, I met him. Say, Allie, you should get back here to visit more often. I mean, with your husband gone and all, there's no reason not to visit more regularly."

I felt the hair on the back of my neck stand up. He had better watch how he brings Thaddeus up, or he could end up with some part of his body broken. He didn't want to make this redhead mad.

"Yes, well, I do have a life back in Maine," I said.

"Your mama's gettin' older now. I'm sure she could use your help around the house, and it would do her good to see you more often," he said, trying to sound helpful.

I could see Alec smirk out of the corner of my eye. "Are you doing social work now, Elmer? I can take care of my mama just fine, thank you."

"Oh, I don't mean to pry or nothin'," he said. "I just thought about how nice it would be to see you more often, is all." He was dressed in a western shirt with pearl buttons and wore a pair of Wranglers that did not complement his figure.

"Well, we'll certainly consider coming out here more often," Alec said, butting in. "This is such a nice little town."

It was my turn to smirk as Elmer slowly turned toward Alec.

"Well now, that would be nice to see you, too. I'm sure you Northerners know how to investigate real good, don't you?" he asked, narrowing his eyes at him.

"Now, Elmer, let's not turn this into a Northerners against Southerners thing. That war was fought long ago," I said, trying not to laugh.

"And as I recall, it didn't turn out so well for you all. Excuse me, y'all," Alec said. He kept a straight face and everything when he said it. I was proud of him.

Elmer's face turned dark red, and for a minute I thought he was going to blow.

"We have no problems investigating our own murders around here," Elmer said through gritted teeth.

"I'm sure you don't," Alec conceded. "John McGinty certainly seems more than competent."

Elmer stood up straighter at the mention of John's name, and I wondered if there was some tension between the two of them. I made a mental note to ask John about it.

"John McGinty? He doesn't understand investigating. He's okay, I mean," Elmer said, catching himself. "It's just that he's a little too laid back. You need to be on top of things to get anything done." He swayed a little bit when he said it, and I wondered if he had perhaps been drinking a little this evening.

"I find being methodical more important than being aggressive. But then, I've only been a detective for around twenty-three years or so," Alec said. "I still have a lot to learn."

I raised one eyebrow at him. He was feeling his oats tonight, and I wondered what had transpired between the two of them the day of Tom's murder.

Elmer narrowed his eyes at Alec but turned to me. "I guess I ought to leave you two to your meal. Ann Marie Cason is over there in the corner, waiting on me. You remember Ann Marie Cason, don't you, Allie?" he grinned at me, waiting for my reply.

It was my turn to grit my teeth. Ann Marie Cason and I had been rivals in high school. Actually, we weren't even rivals. She couldn't stand me, and every time I got a new boyfriend, which wasn't that often, but often enough, she would try to get him to go out with her. It worked a couple of times, so she wasn't my favorite person in the world. Back then, I had spent many a night crying myself to sleep over the boyfriend she had stolen away. Mama would try to make me feel better by saying she was one of those loose girls, and I was better than that. But all I wanted was to be with whatever former boyfriend she had stolen.

"Oh? Is she still in town? Well, I guess if you never make it to college, you don't have much choice but to stay in Goose Bay, do you?" I said with a smile.

The grin left Elmer's face. "She done all right. We both did. I'll talk to you later," he said and spun around, almost lost his balance and pinwheeled his arms to stay on his feet, and then headed back toward the corner table.

I couldn't see that table from where I sat, but I wanted to. I wanted time to have been unkind to Ann Marie Cason. Her blond hair had to be gray by now. Plus, she had tanned excessively in high school. She must have some serious wrinkles by now. It might not have been nice of me to hope she had aged poorly, but I might not have been over losing those boyfriends to her. I would feel badly later for thinking such mean thoughts, but for right now, I was feeling justified. I picked up a piece of garlic toast and bit into it.

"Who's Ann Marie Cason?" Alec asked, reaching for his Mason jar of Cherry Coke.

I sighed and tore into the bread again without having swallowed the first bite. "Boyfriend stealer," I said around the wad of bread in my mouth.

"Really? And did she steal Elmer away from you?" he asked, amused.

I swallowed. "No, she did not. But she did steal some others. The little tramp. I'd like to get a look at her," I said, leaning to the left and trying to see back to the table Elmer had indicated.

Alec chuckled.

"I'm glad you think this is funny," I said.

"Tell, me. How did you end up dating someone named Elmer in the first place?"

I sighed. "Well, back then, he had a little more hair and a little less belly. And he was on the football team. Football is important in a small town. It was every girl's dream to date someone on the football team."

He chuckled. "Oh, the things we did back then. Makes you wonder how we ever made it in the real world, doesn't it?"

I smiled. "It sure does. I bet you have some bad date skeletons in your closet, don't you?" I asked.

"Maybe. But you'll never know," he answered.

"When do I get to meet your family? I bet if we go visit your hometown, I'll get to see some of those skeletons."

He shrugged. "I guess once I'm officially retired, we could make the trip. But we won't be hanging out in any place one of my exes will show up, I assure you."

"That's just wrong," I said, shaking my head. "You've seen the worst I have to offer, and I want to see yours."

Our food came before we could continue the exes discussion, and we dug in. Elmer walked by with Ann Marie, and thankfully they didn't stop by to say hello. I'm sad to report that Ann Marie looked like she had hardly aged since high school. She still had that same knock out body the boys went for back then. Call me small. I don't care. She was a mean boyfriend-stealer.

Chapter Twelve

"I HIGHLY SUSPECT MRS. Anne Beale," I said to Alec as we pulled up to her house. "It's a given."

"Oh? And why is that? Don't tell me. She has a temper?" he asked, turning the minivan off.

"I have no idea if she does or not," I said. "But she's the quiet, mousy type. It's always them. And she cheated for her daughter during the summer reading program at the library."

"Methinks someone sounds bitter," he said and got out of the van.

I got out and hurried over to his side of the van so I could hiss, "No one, and I mean, *no one* was as fast a reader as I was in the sixth grade. You mark my words. We're about to talk to a cheater."

He chuckled. "You need to tone down that competitive nature a little," he said, giving me a quick kiss. He took my hand as we headed toward the front door.

Mrs. Beale lived in a cute pink gingerbread house. The pink was light and sweet and somehow managed to fit the house perfectly. White gingerbread trim set off the front of the house, and there were white wooden planters under the windows. She had put fabric poinsettias in the planters for the Christmas season, and white twinkle lights encircled the windows and planters. It was very small-town cute.

Alec knocked on the door, and we waited. A dog in the backyard barked at the sound of his knocking. Alec put his hand up to knock again when the door slowly opened. Mrs. Beale peeked out from behind the gold chain that kept the door from swinging all the way open.

"Yes?" she asked.

Alec smiled to show he was friendly. "Mrs. Beale, we met several days ago over at Tom Turner's house. I'm Detective Blanchard, and of course, you remember Allie."

Mrs. Beale turned her head to look in my direction and then closed the door. We heard the chain being pulled back, and the door opened again.

"Good afternoon," she said, smoothing down her skirt.

"Good afternoon," Alec said. "May we come in and speak with you? We won't be long."

"Yes, of course," she said and led us to the living room. The room had beige carpet, beige sofas, and a beige ottoman. I had expected a flower explosion, considering the cute façade of the house. There were no Christmas decorations other than a small Christmas tree that sat on an end table in the corner, decorated in silver and red. It looked kind of lonely all by itself.

"Can I get y'all some tea?" she asked after offering us seats.

"That would be wonderful," I said before Alec could answer. I liked being able to stay in someone's house for more than a few minutes. It gave me a better sense of them. Tea would give us a little extra time.

"I'll be right back," she said and left the room.

"It's a cute house," I whispered.

"We could paint your house pink," he answered.

I smiled, trying to imagine my neighbors' reactions to a pink house. I was pretty sure I would get a visit or two with some pointed questions asked.

Mrs. Beal had very little décor in her living room. A couple of family photos hung on one wall and one seascape painting on another. I got up to look at the photos. One was a picture of her daughter Sadie when she won the reading contest in the sixth grade. In the picture, Sadie held up a twelve-inch gold-tone plastic trophy, complete with loving cup on the top. Sadie smiled for all she was worth, her pigtails tied in orange yarn. She wore a denim jumper and blue Keds shoes. I silently snorted. The cheater.

The other photo was one of Mr. and Mrs. Beale on their wedding day. She wore a long white gown that had lace all over. The picture was black and white, and Mrs. Beale beamed behind a long veil. She had been very pretty when she was young. She was still pretty, and I could see why Tom had an interest in her.

"Here we are," Mrs. Beale said, bringing in a tray with a teapot, cups, and sugar and creamer.

"Oh, I was just admiring your wedding picture. You both looked so happy," I said, turning toward her.

She set the tray down on the coffee table. "Oh, thank you. We certainly were. My poor Harold died of pneumonia when Sadie was two. It was a shame. Sadie never really got to know him."

"Oh, I didn't know that," I said, feeling a twinge of guilt for not being kinder to Sadie. We had been such fierce competitors that I never took the time to get to know her.

"Please, help yourselves," she said, motioning toward the tray.

I sat down, and Alec and I made ourselves a cup of tea.

"Did they find the murderer? I heard it was a murder," Mrs. Beale said as she poured a cup of tea.

"We're still investigating," Alec said. "That's why we're here."

A look of fear crossed Mrs. Beale's face. "What?" she asked.

"Oh, no, I mean I just wanted to ask you some questions. We're still looking for whoever did this," Alec reassured her. "I know you said you liked to go over to his house to play Uno once a week, but can you expand on the nature of your relationship?"

Mrs. Beale blushed and looked down at her tea, then slowly took a sip.

"I don't mean to embarrass you, Mrs. Beale," Alec said, then glanced at me.

Way to make her clam up, I thought.

"Well, really, we were just friends. Like I told you before, I went over to supper once a week, and we played card games. Tom wasn't really interested in a relationship," she said. When she looked up, there were tears in her eyes. "I don't know why he didn't want a relationship. Don't most people want that?"

I felt bad. For generations, womankind has been getting the run around in their relationships. Mrs. Beale's generation was no exception.

"I'm sorry, Mrs. Beale," Alec said. "So you were just friends with Tom?"

She nodded. "That's all."

"I see," Alec said, making a note in his notebook. "Tell me, Mrs. Beale, do you know if anyone was angry with Tom?"

Mrs. Beale smiled, stirring her tea. "Well, I can't think of anyone off-hand. Tom was a friend to everyone. Well, almost everyone."

"Oh?" I asked when she didn't immediately continue.

"Well, I don't mean to gossip, but Ida Crawford didn't like Tom. I saw her in the grocery store about a month ago, and she was upset with him," she said, still stirring her tea and nodding her gray head.

"What for?" I asked, trying not to look at Alec.

"She thought he had feelings for her, but when he told her he didn't, she screamed at him. She told him he had been leading her on. Called him a cad."

I did glance sideways at Alec then. Name calling was never a good sign. That was two strikes against Ida. We needed to talk to her.

"I can see where someone who feels like their feelings have been trifled with can feel like they are being used, but it's rarely cause for murder," Alec said, being sane and sensible again.

"Well, you don't know Ida," Mrs. Beale insisted. "She's one of those *loose* women." She whispered the word loose, and I fully expected her to look around to make sure no one else had heard her.

"Was she?" I asked, leaning forward. I still didn't think having orange hair and wearing too much makeup made you a loose woman or a likely murderer, but I was willing to listen.

She nodded. "I heard she and Agnes Jones' husband Earl, had an affair back in 1984."

"Really?" I said. Earl had been a looker back then. I remembered him from Girl Scouts when he would pick up his daughter Marian.

"Oh, yes. I've never trusted the woman."

Alec asked her a few more questions, and we left.

"That's two strikes against Ida," I said when we were in the minivan.

"Two?" he asked, buckling his seat belt.

"Mama suspects her, too."

He chuckled. "Poor Ida Crawford. No one seems to like her."

"Well, you know what they say. Where there's smoke, there's fire," I said.

"And does she have a temper?" he asked.

"Stop it," I said as he pulled away from Mrs. Beale's house. "I don't know if she did it or not. Just seems odd that two people would name her as possibly being Tom's killer."

"That it does," he said. "That it does."

"Let's go to the funeral tomorrow," I said.

"I thought you'd never ask."

Chapter Thirteen

THE PARKING LOT OF the First Baptist Church on Calloway Avenue was packed. Alec had to drive around the block a couple of times to find an open parking spot. I was sitting in the back so Mama could ride up front and not have to wrinkle her dress climbing in the back. I had borrowed one of her dresses since I hadn't planned on going to a funeral while we were visiting. The kids had stayed home since they only knew Tom in passing. I had given them orders to clean grandma's house top to bottom, just to make her feel better.

We got out and made our way inside the church. Tom lay in his casket wearing a red tie and black suit. I went to take a look at him, and he looked better than I ever remembered seeing him.

Ida Crawford stood at the head of his casket, sobbing into a white lace hanky. Her orange hair was done up in a bouffant, and her red lipstick had rubbed off on her hanky. Mama hung back, talking to some of the ladies she knew from church, and I figured she was waiting for Ida to move on. But Ida looked intent on staying put. She had a grip on the edge of the casket.

"Ida," I said in greeting.

She looked up, her black eyeliner smudged under her eyes. She gave me a half-hearted smile. "Allie, how are you, honey?" she said and moved over closer to me and pulled me in close for a hug. Her perfume made breathing nearly impossible as I patiently waited until she had had her fill of hugging.

"There, there," I said when I couldn't find anything else to say. I patted her on the back and turned my head a little so I could get some fresh air.

Finally, she pulled away and held me at arms' length. "You are a sight for sore eyes, girl. Still just as pretty as you ever were. It's a shame we have to see each other under such sad circumstances."

I smiled sympathetically. "Oh, it's good to see you too, Ida. I can't believe this happened to poor Tom. Gosh, I can't imagine who would do such a thing, can you?" I was here, I figured I better make the best of it and see if I could get some information.

She nodded and moved in close again and I was regretting my decision to ask her about the murder when I got another mouthful of that perfume.

"I think it was Anne Beale," she said, nodding knowingly. "You know that woman was at his house at least once a week, trying to get him to pay attention to her. It was probably more than once a week. Wouldn't surprise me if it were nearly every day. You'd think she would have gotten the hint and left him alone."

"Really? I can't imagine why a woman would lower herself that way," I said, shaking my head. "Did she tell you about her going over there?"

"Oh no, Tom did. He said he could hardly stand it when she came around. Said she was a nuisance, and he had no interest in her," she whispered.

Two other ladies stepped up to the casket, and Ida and I took a few steps back.

"That's odd she would persist," I said. "You'd think she would have gotten the hint."

She nodded again. "She was always an odd one, if you ask me. I think she finally had enough of his rejecting her, although knowing Tom he was sweet as he could be about it. And then she killed him," she said, her voice cracking on the last part. She blew her nose into her handkerchief.

I clucked my tongue and shook my head. "It's a terrible shame," I said.

More people began streaming toward the casket, so I excused myself and headed back to the last row of pews where Alec sat, waiting. When Mama saw Ida leave the casket area for her own pew, she got in line to see Tom.

I leaned over toward Alec and whispered. "Guess who just fingered Mrs. Beale for the murder?"

He chuckled. "I can only guess."

"Seems Tom told Ida that he couldn't stand Anne Beale coming around every week. Said she was a nuisance."

He sighed. "Either some ladies are telling some tall tales, or Tom was quite the man about town."

"My money's on Tom," I said.

"Mine might be, too."

I scanned the room and recognized most of the faces from my youth, but there were a number of people I didn't recognize at all. The landscape of Goose Bay was changing, and I was missing it. For a few moments, I wondered what it would be like to move back home. It filled me with happiness until I considered what I would miss in Sandy Harbor. My daughter going to college nearby for one. And Lucy and Ed for two. And everything and everyone else I had known over the past twenty-plus years. I sighed. I would be homesick no matter where I lived.

"Do you think his daughter will show?" I asked, looking around again.

"I don't know. People behave peculiarly when grieving. She may say she doesn't care about him, but it most likely isn't true. He was her father, after all," he said.

Mama made her way back to our pew, dabbing at her eyes with a tissue, and I felt bad for her. She stopped and hugged a younger woman, and then continued back to where we were and sat next to me. I put my arm around her shoulders, and she leaned over and laid her head on my shoulder. I didn't say anything. There was nothing to say.

Alec nudged me a few minutes before the service was scheduled to begin, and I looked over at the door just as Leslie Warren walked through it. Staggered was more like it. The red floral dress she wore was two sizes too big for her, and she wore purple shoes with it that had seen much better days. She was a mess, and I felt bad for her, too. I hoped she would be okay. She appeared to be alone, and I wondered who the people were on the front row pew. I couldn't remember if Tom had more family in town, and Mama hadn't mentioned any.

"Mama, who are those people in the first row? Tom's kin? I don't recognize them," I whispered.

She sat up and dabbed at her eyes again. "Yes, that's his sister Pamela, I think you met her years ago, and his brother Steven. The younger ones are nieces and nephews, I think. I think they live in Mobile."

I couldn't remember Pamela, but I could see a family resemblance in one of the young ladies. She had to be Leslie's cousin. Leslie continued down the aisle, and people stepped aside.

I felt myself cringe as she stood at the casket looking at her dead father. I could imagine all the pain and regret going through her mind right then. She held onto the side of the casket and leaned in toward him. My stomach dropped. She wouldn't kiss him, would she? Or worse?

I glanced at Alec, who was intently watching Leslie. Leslie leaned in even closer and whispered something to Tom, and then stood up straight.

"I hate you," she said very clearly and loud enough to be heard back where we sat.

The room went silent. Leslie's hands still gripped the side of the casket, and her face turned red, as she leaned over again and spit on her father.

Alec was on his feet and at her side before anyone else could get to her. I trailed behind him to help. The buzz in the room grew louder, and I hoped we wouldn't have a riot on our hands.

"Leslie, why don't you come sit with Allie and me?" he said in a low, calm tone.

A big burly looking cousin stepped toward Leslie, and Alec held a hand up to stop him. Leslie didn't turn toward Alec but continued staring at her father. Her fingers gripped the edge of the casket.

"She needs to leave," the cousin said in a low voice.

"You need to sit down," Alec warned.

Alec had one arm protectively around Leslie's shoulders and asked her to come sit with us again. I stood nearby, not knowing what to do. I went to the cousin and said, "It's okay. It will be fine."

He looked at me, anger burning in his eyes, but he took several steps back. I had no idea how the family dynamic had been before Leslie had a falling out with her father, but clearly, things hadn't been good for a while, and this wasn't helping things.

"Come on, Leslie," Alec murmured. Leslie swayed on her feet and then let go of the side of the casket, and Alec led her to the back pew.

I followed them and went around to the other side. Alec sat her between us. Mama sat on my other side. I took Leslie's hand as she began to sob, then put my arm around her shoulders.

Mama looked at me, then turned her attention to the pastor as he began the service. Tears streamed down my cheeks as I held Leslie. My heart was breaking, but I didn't know how to help her. Some things were too complicated to fix for someone else.

Chapter Fourteen

DECEMBER 18TH WAS THE night of the annual Christmas carnival. It was held at the high school gym, and nearly the whole town had turned out for it. My sister Shelby, and my brother Jake had arrived earlier, and we had spent some time catching up.

There would be raffles at the carnival, and I had volunteered to make a contribution. I had baked a fresh batch of gingerbread men and a small gingerbread house, and arranged them in a gift basket and wrapped them in clear cellophane. All funds went to the high school sports teams to buy new equipment. The city had had to make cutbacks, and this was a great opportunity to help the kids.

At 6:00 we headed out to the carnival.

The gym was lit up with floodlights on the outside and Christmas lights on the inside. People milled about, hot chocolate or coffee in hand, catching up with friends and neighbors they hadn't seen in a while. The gym was filled with booths, where for a dollar, you could play games and win a prize. There were tables of baked goods for sale as well as crafts. Christmas cheer was in the air, and it felt good to be here.

"Let's get hot cocoa, Allie," Shelby said. Shelby was twelve years younger than I was. An oops child, and she had been my pride and joy growing up. She was the best gift my parents could have given me. My twelve-year-old self had taken her as my own, when Mama would allow it.

"Sounds good," I said, and we went and got in line.

Shelby had strawberry blond hair, and other than the fact that mine was a darker red and I was older, we could have passed as twins. She lived a couple of hours away in Gaston and worked at a café.

Jake was three years older and newly divorced. His wife had been unable to have children, and he had been fine with being childless, but one day his now ex-wife had told him she wanted to be with a younger man. One who had three motherless children, and she left. He had time on his hands, and he visited Mama as frequently as he could. Earlier he had mentioned moving back to Goose Bay, and I hoped he would. It would be good for Mama, and probably for him as well. I could tell he was lonely being out on his own after twenty years of marriage.

"So is it true, what happened at Tom's funeral?" Shelby whispered, looking over her shoulder.

I nodded. "I'm afraid so. It's sad. I wish they could have made up before he died."

"It really is sad. But you have to admit, Leslie brought some of it on herself," she said, and we scooted up as the line got shorter.

"What do you mean?" I asked.

"Oh, you know. She has a history of drug use. Her father wanted her to go into rehab, but she didn't want to. He had to bail her out of jail a time or two. Her mind isn't always clear, I don't think, and she tells some tall tales about what happened between them," she said.

"Yes, but I think the real issue was that Tom dated other women while her mother was in the nursing home," I said.

She looked at me. "Case in point. No, he didn't date other women while his wife was in a nursing home. His wife died about a week after she went into the nursing home, and he was by her side."

I looked at her wide-eyed. "Are you sure?"

She nodded. "Yes, my friend Christa worked at the nursing home when she was there. Said she died within a week of arriving. Natural causes."

I stared at her. "Then why did Leslie say he had dated other women? Why has she been angry all these years?"

She shrugged. "I told you. She's had a drug problem for years."

That was something to ponder. I had been sure she was telling us the truth. We got our hot cocoa, as well as some for Jake, Mama, and Alec. The kids had wandered off to look at things on their own, so they were out of luck.

"Mama, did Tom date women while his wife was in the nursing home?" I whispered when we got back.

Alec looked at me, and then at Mama. "No, why would he do that? He loved his wife."

"She died right after she went into the nursing home," Shelby repeated, and Mama nodded her head in agreement.

I looked at Alec.

"Maybe we should go talk to Leslie again," he said.

"I guess so," I agreed.

"Hi, y'all," John McGinty said, walking up with his wife, Cara.

"Cara!" I screeched and hugged her tightly to me. "How are you?"

"Oh, Allie, it's so good to see you. I'm good. You look great!" she exclaimed.

"Oh my goodness, I've missed you!" I said, releasing her to take a good look at her. "You haven't aged a bit!" And she hadn't. She was still cute as ever, with her long brown hair and green eyes that sparkled.

"Oh, please. Now you're telling tall tales. But you do look the same," she said. "I can't believe we didn't just graduate high school. I don't know where the time goes."

"Me either. I have kids around here somewhere. I need to introduce you to them," I said.

"Mine are coming in on the twenty-third for Christmas. We'll have to get together before you leave. I left that hippie back on the farm in Idaho. It's good to be back home, and of course, I found, or rather, rediscovered a certain John McGinty," she said, looking at her husband.

John blushed and looked away. He was still that shy math nerd.

I introduced Cara to Alec, and he smiled at her and shook her hand.

"John told me you were helping out in Tom Turner's murder," she said. "I just can't believe that happened. I don't know what's going on around here."

"It is a shame," Alec agreed. He looked at John. "Did you know Leslie Warren is saying that her father Tom Turner abandoned her mother at a nursing home and was dating other women? She said that's why they were estranged."

"I've heard different things. Sometimes it's hard to sort out fact from fiction in a small town," John said.

Alec looked at me. "That's the truth."

I narrowed my eyes at him.

We stood and talked for a few minutes when Jennifer walked up to us. She took my arm and pulled me aside.

"Hey, Jen, I want to introduce you to someone," I said, before noticing the wild-eyed look on her face. "What's up, sis?"

"Mom, there's this woman following me," she said and glanced over her shoulder.

I looked in the direction she was looking, but only saw people enjoying the carnival. "Who?" I asked.

"I don't know. I don't see her now," she said, searching the crowd.

"How do you know she was following you? There are a lot of people here. Maybe she was just looking at the same booths you were," I said.

"No, I swear, every time I turn around, she's there," she said, still looking. "Except for now."

"What did she look like?" I asked.

"She was wearing a black trench coat and had dark curly hair. I think she was older, but she didn't get that close to me so I could see. Mom, it's creepy," she whined.

"Where are your brother and Sarah? You should stay with them, or stay here with us," I said.

"I don't know, I lost track of them when I played the hoop game over there," she said, pointing to a booth.

I continued scanning the crowd but didn't see anyone in a black trench coat. I didn't want to say that Jennifer was being paranoid because she was my sensitive child, but I didn't see anyone behaving the least bit odd. She could have seen something, but I couldn't imagine how she could tell with all the people moving around. Whoever she had seen could easily have been moving from booth to booth, playing games, and visiting with people and just happened to be following behind her.

"It'll be all right," I said and hugged her. "Come over here and meet my best friend from high school."

I introduced Cara to Jennifer, and we walked around the carnival, with Jennifer sticking close. She looked over her shoulder frequently while Alec looked at me questioningly.

"I'll tell you later," I whispered.

Chapter Fifteen

"ALL RIGHT, I'M DEPENDING on you to win that Rudolph for me," I told Alec as we stood in front of the ring toss. Small goldfish bowls sat on Styrofoam rings that floated in a large pool of water. Alec needed to toss a ring onto five of them to win the Rudolph for me. Otherwise, we were taking a goldfish home with us.

"All right, I've got this," he said, warming up his arm.

"I want Bambi," Jennifer said, looking at the stuffed animal hanging from the top of the booth.

"You hear that? You've got two stuffed animals to win," I told him. "That arm better be strong."

He grinned, keeping his eyes on the goldfish bowls. "No problem," he said and let a ring go. It landed perfectly over the bowl, and he laughed. "See?"

"I see," I said. "Now don't miss this one," I said as he let another loose.

It landed squarely around another bowl.

"Wow, look at that," I said. I kept an eye out for the woman in a black trench coat, but couldn't find her. Jennifer would look at the crowd every few minutes, scanning nervously. I still wondered if she had imagined things, but she seemed so sure some woman had been following her.

Alec tossed the next two rings, and they sank perfectly around the fishbowls. "One more and you've got a Rudolph," he said and let the last one go. It hit the top of a fishbowl and bounced off, sinking sadly into the pool of water.

"Oh, no!" Jennifer and I howled together. "You missed!"

"You get one of the smaller animals for four rings around the bowls," the man behind the booth said.

"Which one do you want?" Alec asked me.

"Oh, no. I want Rudolph. You'll have to try again," I said, leaning on the front of the booth.

The man running the booth handed Alec a small stuffed cat. "You still get a prize anyway," he said.

"What do we do with the cat?" he asked me. "It's awful cute. Are you sure you don't want it instead of Rudolph?"

I grabbed the orange striped kitty from the man and handed it to a little girl walking by. Her eyes lit up, and her mother reminded her to say thank you.

Ten minutes and thirty dollars later, we had our Rudolph and Bambi. Alec looked at me as the man behind the booth handed us our prizes. "We could have gone to Walmart and spent half that amount."

"Yes, but where's the fun in that?" I asked him.

He sighed and rolled his eyes. The man had no clue about fun.

I looked up just as Elmer walked in with Ann Marie, and I groaned.

"Who's that?" Jennifer asked, looking in the direction I was looking.

"Ex-boyfriend and the girl that use to steal most girls' boyfriends," I said.

"Mom, she's not even pretty," she said.

Have I mentioned how much I love that girl?

"Thanks, honey, but she is pretty. Just not nice," I said.

"And how could you date that guy? You should be embarrassed," she said, curling her lip.

"Gee, thanks. Back then he was on the football team. It was a long time ago," I said.

"So. Not cool, Mom," she said.

Elmer made a beeline toward me. I debated whether I could run to the nearest bathroom fast enough, but he had a determined look on his face, and I figured he'd probably wait outside for me.

"Hey, Allie," he said, looking at me and then at Jennifer. Somehow he forgot Alec was standing there.

"Me and Ann Marie are going to get married," he said, grinning at me like a loon.

"Oh really?" I said. "Congratulations." I tried to sound enthusiastic, but I probably didn't.

"Hey, Allie, haven't seen you around in a while," Ann Marie said, catching up to Elmer. Her hair was teased like it was 1987, and she wore a skirt that was way too short for the weather.

"Hey, Ann Marie. I bet you're excited about getting married," I said, trying to be nice.

"Yes, I am. Maybe I'll have you make my wedding cake. I know you bake a little," she said. "Oh, wait a minute. A wedding cake won't be too hard for you, will it?"

I could feel anger rising on the inside of me. "I'm pretty sure I could handle a wedding cake," I said, trying not to spit poison with my words.

"Who's this pretty little lady?" Elmer asked, still looking at Jennifer.

"My daughter, Jennifer," I said, and introduced them.

"Well, she sure takes after her mama," Elmer said, looking her up and down. I wanted to punch him, and if he didn't quit looking at Jennifer that way, it would happen.

"Thanks, we need to get going," I said, and turned away, taking Alec's hand.

"Hey Elmer, John said you were getting some evidence processed for the Turner case. Where are you on that?" Alec asked.

I smiled. He had said it just because he knew it would irritate him, but I gave him a warning look, only because I felt like it was my obligation.

"I don't see where that's your business, seeing as how it isn't your case," he said, standing tall.

"Now, you know John asked me to help out. There's no need to get riled up. That's a Southern word, isn't it? Riled?" Alec asked, ignoring my warning look.

I wanted to reach over and pinch him, but I knew it wouldn't do any good. He was having fun, and there wasn't much I could do about it.

Elmer's face went red. "I have already submitted the evidence for testing," he said through gritted teeth. "Now, if you'll excuse me, I have things to do." With that, he grabbed Ann Marie by the arm and pulled her back through the crowd.

That would teach him to come over and talk to me. I hoped. I would be happy if he never talked to me again.

"So, you're making their wedding cake?" Alec asked with a grin.

"I don't think so," I said curtly. "I'd rather have honey poured over me and be staked to an anthill."

"He's creepy," Jennifer said and shuddered. "I can't believe you dated him."

"Me either."

"JENNIFER SAID THERE was a woman following her at the carnival," I whispered to Alec as we stood on the front porch and gazed at the moon. It was cold out, but the moon was beautiful. I could stare at that moon all night, even if it meant freezing my nose off.

"Who?" he asked, looking down at me. He was a good ten inches taller than I was, and I had to look up at him.

I shrugged. "She doesn't know anyone here. She just said she had a black trench coat on and had dark curly hair. She thought she was older, but she didn't get that close to her. I don't know why anyone would follow her."

"I remember a woman with a black trench coat," he said, still looking at me. "Why did she think she was following her?"

"I'm not sure. Jennifer can be very emotional, so I kind of thought she might be just a little paranoid is all. She said every time she turned around, the woman was there. I pointed out the woman could have just been following the crowd along, like everyone else, but she insisted she was following her. Did the woman you saw have dark curly hair?"

"I'm not sure. I just glanced at her. I remember the coat and not much else. I wasn't looking for anyone, and the only reason she caught my attention was because of the coat. Something about it struck me as different. Or maybe it just seemed like an odd choice for outerwear, given the weather was dry and cold."

"Well, I told her to stick with her brother and Sarah, or us. I never did see that woman. I kept looking for her after she told me about her."

"Tell her not to go out alone, and if she sees her, she needs to call me," he said.

"I will," I said. "You think it was the killer?"

"I have no idea. But she trusted her instincts, and that's good. It doesn't hurt to be careful."

"Okay," I said, laying my head against his chest. As much as I loved getting to visit with my mama, I really wanted to go home. There had been entirely too much excitement since we had arrived, and I was ready for some peace and quiet.

Tom Turner's house stood dark in the moonlight, and it made me sad. Christmas should be a happy time, not one of grieving. I worried about Leslie and thought I needed to visit her again. Maybe I would invite her to Christmas dinner if she was going to be spending it alone.

Chapter Sixteen

THE WEATHER GOT COLDER, with a heavy frost covering the ground in the morning. Alec and I got up early to get a long run in before breakfast. My running pants felt snug, and I reminded myself to cut back on Mama's buttermilk biscuits.

The ground was slippery as we headed for the woods, and I almost lost my footing. Alec reached out and grabbed my jacket sleeve to steady me.

"I got it," I said. We were slowly jogging to warm up as the sun rose above the trees. It was a glorious sight with the bright, clear blue sky above us. "I love this place."

"It is beautiful," Alec agreed. "By the way, how is Lucy doing?"

"She's good. Trying to figure out this thing from Maine, and Dixie is doing fine," I said between breaths. Dixie was my cat, and when I got home I knew I'd get an earful for leaving him for so long.

He chuckled. "So glad to hear it." He was wearing gloves and a light jacket to stay warm while running.

We ran in silence for a while, just enjoying the sights. The birds in the trees slowly woke up and began their songs and a rabbit popped its head out of its burrow. I wondered how people in big cities managed to survive in their concrete worlds, almost devoid of God's creation.

"Faster?" Alec asked after we had been running for ten minutes.

"Yeah," I said, nodding.

The cold bit at my cheeks as we picked up our pace. I glanced at the pace and heart rate monitor on my arm. We were making good time with an eight-minute mile, but I wanted to go faster. There was something freeing about being out here in the wild that made me want to run at my fastest pace.

As a girl, I had spent many afternoons and weekends exploring these woods and I had known them intimately. I explored mostly on my own, but sometimes with Jake or a friend. Jake had shown me how to catch frogs and fish in the pond on the other side of the woods, and we had grown close, with me looking up to my big brother. I missed those days.

"Over here," I said to Alec, and I took him down a now overgrown path, deeper into the woods. Years ago the path had been cleared, but in the years since then, it had grown over with weeds and grass. There were some bushes that I didn't remember seeing back then, and for a few minutes, I wondered if I had taken a wrong turn. But then I saw the old oak tree that had been split by lightning when I was ten. I was amazed that it still stood, leeching out life where it could.

We increased our pace to a seven and a half minute mile, and the woods whipped by. My eyes watered in the cold and I brushed the moisture away with the back of my gloved hand. The trees were barren of leaves, having dropped to the ground earlier. The carpet of leaves we ran through crunched under our feet, protesting our presence.

Alec pulled ahead of me by a few paces, and I increased my pace to match his. His longer legs had an unfair advantage over mine. He glanced sideways at me and grinned.

"Ready to go harder?" he said between breaths.

"Yeah, sure," I breathed out. My breathing sounded like a freight train now, and my lungs burned with the cold, but I was always game to run harder, longer, or faster.

He turned on the speed and I pushed myself to keep up with him, my lungs protesting.

In a few moments, my body was airborne. I hit the ground with a dull thud, my head spinning, and the breath in my lungs gone. I lay in the leaves, trying to figure out what had happened and why I was on the cold hard ground.

"Allie! Are you okay?" Alec panted, kneeling beside me.

I stared at the small pile of leaves in front of me, confused.

"Allie?" Alec asked.

I could hear the panic in his voice, and I looked up at him. "Hey," I whispered, trying to catch my breath.

"Are you okay?" he asked, breathing in hard.

"I... I think so," I said, mentally assessing my body.

"Let me help you to a sitting position," he said and reached his arms around me, turning me over. He gently helped me to a sitting position.

My head was still spinning and my right knee was throbbing.

"I must have tripped," I said, looking in the direction we had come from.

He smiled. "Maybe running fast through leaves on unfamiliar ground wasn't the brightest thing to do," he said.

"Maybe not. I use to run through these woods all the time as a girl," I said.

"I'm sure it's overgrown since then, and become a running hazard, as we've seen," he said with a chuckle.

"Well, it was fun while it lasted. But my knee really hurts."

"Let me see," he said and gently pulled up the leg of my running pants to expose my knee. Blood trickled out of a deeply skinned patch the size of a grapefruit. "Ouch. That looks painful."

"It's going to hurt more when the adrenaline wears off," I said.

"Let's see if you can walk on it." He put his arm around my waist and helped me to my feet. "Is it bad?" he asked when I winced.

I took a couple of steps on it. "Not as bad as it could be. I think it's mostly the scraped skin, and not anything deeper. At least I hope not."

"Good. I'm sure it'll bruise, but that's easier to get over than damage done to the joint." He helped me hobble back in the direction we had come from.

"I guess that's what I hit," I said, pointing to an exposed tree root reaching across the path we had been running on. "It must have been covered by the leaves."

"I guess that will teach us to run wild and free in the woods, eh?"

I laughed. "That'll do it. I'm getting too old to take a fall like that. I am going to be hurting tomorrow morning."

We hobbled a few more steps, and I saw something glint in the morning sun. "Hey, what's that?"

Alec went over and moved some more leaves and exposed what looked like a dagger lying there.

"Well," Alec said, kneeling down. "It looks like we may have discovered the murder weapon."

"Really?" I asked, hobbling over to him.

The handle on the dagger was bejeweled with red and green rhinestones and it had what looked to be an eight-inch blade, covered in dried blood.

"Wow. That looks nasty," I said leaning closer.

"It sure does," he said and took his phone out of his pocket and started taking pictures of it where it was laying.

"Those red and green rhinestones don't make me feel very jolly. Do you think Tom picked it out for its Christmas colors?" I asked him.

He chuckled. "You think of the oddest things sometimes."

"I can't help it," I said. "But I'm not odd, I'm creative."

"Maybe the victim bought himself a Christmas present," he said. "I wish I had my notebook with me."

I smirked. "I thought it was attached to your wrist."

He picked the dagger up with his gloved hand after taking pictures of the entire area, being careful to not disturb the blood on the blade.

"We'll have to send it in to make sure it's Tom's blood, but I'd put money on it," he said. "Come on, let's get you home."

I hobbled over to him and he put his arm around my waist to help me. The other hand held the dagger, and I couldn't help but glance at it from time to time as we walked. What an awful way to die.

We had gone about five miles and it was a long walk home. I wondered who could have wielded such a menacing weapon and plunged it into Tom's chest. I shivered. I couldn't imagine doing something like that, and I couldn't fathom what must have gone through the killer's mind that allowed them to take a life.

"I'll be glad when this whole thing is over," I said after we had walked in silence for a while.

"Me too," he said. "When we get to the road, we can call someone to come get us if your knee is hurting badly enough."

"I think it's okay. It's kind of gone numb from the cold at this point," I said. "The road isn't far from Mama's house, anyway."

I hoped the dagger would yield the killer's fingerprints so this could be put to rest, just as Tom had been put to rest a couple of days earlier.

Chapter Seventeen

"OW, OW, OW!" I SAID as Mama dabbed on the Merthiolate. "Seriously, Mama? Have you had that same bottle since I was nine?"

"No, this is the one I had when Shelby was nine," she said. She looked at Alec. "She was always a big baby."

Alec chuckled. "I'm not sure that I blame her for complaining."

I blew on my knee. A large dark bruise was spreading beneath the scrape and I knew I would be sore all over by tomorrow morning.

I ate a biscuit with butter and honey on it while Alec put the dagger in a two-gallon Ziploc bag.

"Good thing I buy those big ones," Mama murmured, trying not to look at the dagger.

"Let's go," Alec said, grabbing a biscuit.

I hobbled out to the minivan and got in. I needed coffee, but it would have to wait.

ELMER WAS LEANING ON the reception desk at the sheriff's office, flirting with the receptionist. The smile left his face when he saw Alec walk through the door. I glanced down at Alec's hand and noted he had draped his jacket over the hand that carried the bag with the dagger in it.

"Good morning, Elmer," Alec said brightly.

Elmer sneered at him, then grudgingly said, "Morning."

"Is John around?" I asked.

Elmer looked at me, and didn't answer for a moment, then changed his mind and said, "He's in his office."

"Great. Thanks. We'll go on back and say hello to him," I said, and we went on down the hall.

When we were out of Elmer's sight, I looked back at Alec and gave him a big smile. "He doesn't like you for some reason," I whispered.

"I can't imagine why," he said innocently.

I snickered and knocked on John's door when we got to it.

"Come in," he called from the other side.

John's desk was covered in file folders and papers. I wondered which one was Tom's, but I wasn't going to ask. I didn't want to see any pictures.

"Hey, y'all," he said, smiling. "What's up?"

Alec held up the bag with the dagger. "Possible murder weapon."

"Wow. Where'd you find that?" he said, wide-eyed.

Alec laid it on his desk and we took a seat. "Well, my graceful girlfriend here took a spill during our morning run, and she saw it when the sun shone on it."

"Are you all right, Allie?" he asked, turning to me.

"Yes, just a scrape and a bruise or two," I said. "It's kind of weird. That thing just laying out there."

"Where was it exactly?" John asked.

"About five miles out from the murder scene, deep in the woods. I think it must have been covered in dead leaves, but Miss Graceful here might have uncovered it in her fall," Alec said with a grin.

I gave him a look. If it wasn't for all the leaves, I wouldn't have tripped over the tree root and fallen, and he knew it.

"Wow, what a find," John said, examining it through the bag. "I hope it yields some useable fingerprints."

"Why would it just be laying out there? Wouldn't you think the killer would have buried it?" I asked. "Or taken it with them?"

"You would think so. But they may have panicked. It's hard to second-guess a criminal. They don't do things normal people do because their minds are always trying to figure out what might go wrong and cause them to be caught," John said.

"I'm going to stick with it being a regular person and not an expert criminal. It's less complicated," I said. It still amazed me that anyone could murder another human being. I had never even been angry enough for it to cross my mind.

"I've got a number of pictures of the area where we found it," Alec said. "I'll send them to your phone. I can show you where I found it if you want to have a closer look at the area."

"That's a great help," John said, nodding. "I'm glad it was you two that came across it. It's odd, but the crime lab said the broken Christmas plate we found at the scene only had Tom

Turner's prints on it. You would have thought the person that made or brought the cookies would have left prints behind."

"Do you think it was premeditated then?" I asked. "They planned on killing him and wore gloves?"

"It's a possibility," John said. "I can see someone wearing gloves to bring the cookies to him since it's cold. But the baker wouldn't have worn them, I wouldn't think."

Alec nodded, thinking. "Part of me feels like it was a crime of passion, but it's hard to know to this point."

"I wonder why he was holding a candy cane when he was killed?" I asked.

John shrugged. "Maybe he just happened to be holding it and got so scared when he realized he was going to be stabbed, that he just never turned loose of it."

"Maybe the killer gave it to him as a gift and then turned on him. A girlfriend. I'm voting crime of passion," I said. It seemed obvious to me.

"Passion means rage, and possibly jealousy, considering Tom had a reputation as a, um, ladies' man," Alec said. "I'm leaning toward that, too."

"I once read of a woman that killed her lover by stabbing him with knitting needles," John said. "She found out he had cheated on her with a woman that crocheted and the fact that she crocheted made her angrier than the cheating, so she stabbed him repeatedly with knitting needles. She told the police she needed him to understand that crocheting was an inferior form of craft."

"Wow," I said. "Haven't people heard of just breaking up?"

"Not when they're unhinged to begin with," Alec said.

I was glad I wasn't in law enforcement. I couldn't imagine all the crazy people they had to deal with in the line of duty.

"John, I thought I'd mention something. The other night when we were at the Christmas carnival, Jennifer said there was a woman in a black trench coat with short, dark curly hair. She said she was following her and it freaked her out. Did you happen to notice anyone like that?" I asked.

He frowned, thinking back. "I really don't remember. Did she say she had any contact with her before?"

"No, Jennifer doesn't know anyone here. She hasn't gone out much after having discovered Tom's body. She's the sensitive sort, and it really upset her."

"I thought I had seen the woman, but I can't be sure," Alec added. "I don't remember seeing anyone that was behaving suspiciously."

John shook his head. "I wish I'd have known about it at the time. I might have seen her."

"I'm sorry, I guess I should have said something to you guys. After she told me, I kept an eye out for her, but I didn't see her. The rest of the evening Jennifer hung out with Alec and me. She was upset over it. I don't know why I didn't mention it to you both," I said, kicking myself mentally.

"Maybe it was nothing," Alec said. "Like you said, the woman might just have been making the circuit of booths and Jennifer thought she was following her. She's been so shaken by finding Tom's body, she's actually been nice to me."

I snorted. "Well, some good came of it, I guess. I think you're right though. I think she's on edge."

"Well, let me know if she notices anything else," John said.

"Is there anything new with the case?" Alec asked.

John sighed. "Just that Leslie Warren was arrested for public intoxication. She was screaming at one of Tom's girlfriends at the Piggly Wiggly. Accusing her of being the killer. It's sad. I had a talk with her when she sobered up. Suggested she get into rehab and try to not waste the rest of her life."

"What did she say?" I asked.

"She agreed it would be good and said she would look into it. I gave her some phone numbers. I don't know that she'll do it though," he said. "It's a hard change to make."

I nodded. "It's sad."

"Who was the girlfriend she was screaming at?" Alec asked.

"Charlotte Moody," John said. "Do you know her?"

I nodded. "She's the aunt of a friend from high school. I wonder why she thought it was her?" I asked. "I mean, I wonder if there's something there, and she felt like she was more likely the killer than someone else."

John shrugged. "She never said. I think she just happened to run into her at the wrong time is all."

I sighed. "Probably so."

"Well, John, we appreciate your time," Alec said, standing up. "And I'd appreciate your keeping us updated. If Jennifer sees that woman, we'll certainly let you know."

John stood up to see us out. "Well, I appreciate y'all finding that dagger. And I agree, it's most likely the murder weapon. It looks like something Tom would have had in his collection."

We said our goodbyes and headed out to the minivan. Elmer was nowhere to be seen, and the receptionist didn't look up from her computer screen as we passed.

"Well, hopefully that dagger has what we need to arrest the killer," I said once we were outside the sheriff's station.

Alec nodded in agreement. This thing needed to be put to rest.

Chapter Eighteen

"GOT IT," I SAID, HOLDING up the key to Tom's house. Alec had wanted to put Tom's little black book back where we found it. "We'll be right back," I called over my shoulder.

"Maybe we should have taken copies of it to give to John," I said to Alec.

"What for? It's an address book. There wasn't anything interesting in it," he said.

"Maybe. But I bet the killer's name is in there," I said as we walked next door. The sun was setting, and it would be dark shortly.

"Probably so, but so are a lot of others," he said. "I bet the white pages of the phone book has the killer's name in it, too."

"Yeah, yeah," I said.

He unlocked Tom's front door and let us in. It looked the same as when we left it the other day. "I wonder who's going to come and clean his stuff out? Don't you think they'll sell the house?" I asked.

"I would imagine. I don't know if he would have left it to his daughter or not, considering their relationship," he mused. He went to the little table in the hall and opened the drawer. "That's odd."

"What?" I asked.

"I don't remember these keys in this drawer."

I went over and looked at the drawer. "He had relatives in town for the funeral. Maybe they came by the house and found them and put them in there?"

"I suppose. I wonder what they go to, and why someone wanted them," he said, placing the book back in the drawer and closing it.

"I'll go water his plant," I said, remembering the Elephant Ears.

I opened the cupboard and took a glass out and went to the sink. The water was ice cold when I turned the tap on and filled the glass. The plant looked the same, and I wondered if I should take it to my mother. She might have liked it to remember Tom by. I wondered if that would be classified as stealing or if anyone would care. I poured a little water on the plant and dumped the rest.

I dried the glass on the dishtowel hanging near the sink and put it back in the cupboard. Death was a terrible thing. Murder was even worse.

I hobbled back into the living room and stopped. Alec was looking through a magazine rack.

"Want to know what happened in 1989? He has a Time magazine if you do," he said, thumbing through the magazine rack beside the hall table, and then looked up at me. The smile left his face. "What's wrong?"

I frowned. "I'm not sure. Something's different." I suddenly had this eerie feeling about the place. More so than the first time we had searched the house.

He straightened up, and his eyes went around the room. "What's different?"

Then it hit me. "The vacuum. It's gone. It was sitting right there next to the wall."

He went to the hall closet and opened it. "It's not in here."

"Maybe he kept it someplace else," I said and went to the guest bedroom. I couldn't shake the feeling that I was trespassing in someone's house and they might come home to discover me at any moment. I pulled open the closet, but it only had the few items of clothing it had in it before. I closed the door and looked around. Everything seemed the same. Except... I smelled lemons. My heart pounded in my chest. We *were* trespassing.

I hurried back into the living room as Alec was coming out of the master bedroom. "It's not in there."

"Not in the guest bedroom, either," I said. "And I smell lemons in there."

He looked at me. "Lemons?"

I nodded.

He went into the den while I checked the bathroom. I looked under the sink, but the same cleaning supplies and toiletries were there from the other day. I headed back to the den. I suddenly wanted Alec near me.

"Maybe we should go," I whispered.

"Yeah, in a minute," he said, looking over the weapons collection. "Something's not right."

"What?" I asked, looking at the weapons displayed there.

He pulled his phone out of his pocket and started swiping. He stopped and tapped on a picture and I peered at his phone. A picture of the wall we were standing in front of was on his phone.

He looked up at the wall. "There's a dagger missing," he said.

"Are you sure?" I asked.

"Yeah, see?" he said and made the picture larger. A large dagger with blue jewels on the handle had hung on the wall at the bottom of the display.

"When did you take that picture?" I asked.

"The day of the murder. I took a lot of pictures and texted them to John. John was outside, taking pictures of the crime scene, so I took pictures inside the house," he said. "Do you remember if that dagger was there when we were here last?"

I stared at the spot, trying to make myself remember. "Maybe?" I said. "Yes. No, wait. No, I don't remember."

He stared at it. "I don't either. There were several missing on the day of the murder as well as when we were in here. I didn't think to look at the pictures to see if anything had changed. I just assumed it hadn't. Rookie mistake."

"You can't blame yourself. You can't think of everything," I said.

"I have enough experience that I should think of most," he said.

"What would someone want with a dagger and a vacuum?" I asked.

"I have no idea," he said. "Unless the killer vacuumed up some evidence and became paranoid that we would check it. And you know what?"

"What?"

"We should have." He sighed heavily. "Let's take one more look around, and then we'll go."

We looked through the pictures on his phone and compared them to what was here now, going through each room and carefully looking at everything.

"There doesn't seem to be anything else missing," Alec said when we had gone through the entire house again.

"It kind of creeps me out, knowing someone came back for that dagger," I said.

"Yeah, I know what you mean," Alec said, still scanning the living room.

The air was pierced by a scream and Alec and I looked at each other wide-eyed.

"That's Jennifer!" I said, but Alec was already out the front door.

I stumbled after him, trying to ignore the pain that shot through my knee, as Jennifer screamed again.

Chapter Nineteen

I COULDN'T KEEP UP with Alec as he ran across the lawn and back to my mother's house. I caught sight of his backside as he swung the front gate open. Thad burst through the front door, running around the side of the house.

"Thad!" Alec shouted.

Thad looked over his shoulder but kept running. Alec followed after him.

I got to the front steps and hesitated. Did I follow Alec and Thad, or go to Jennifer? I decided the guys could handle themselves. Alec had a gun, after all. I took the front steps two at a time and ran through the front door.

Jennifer, Mama, and Sarah stood in the middle of the living room, holding on to one another.

"What happened?" I gasped.

Tears streamed down Jennifer's face. "Someone was at the window. Someone's out there!"

"Oh," I said and went to them. "It'll be okay. Alec and Thad will find whoever it was."

"What about Thad? Whoever it was might be armed and Thad doesn't have a weapon to protect himself," Sarah asked, her voice cracking.

"It'll be okay," I repeated, hoping it was so. "Alec has a gun, and he was right behind Thad."

We stood and held each other for a while, listening for what was going on outside. The silence was deafening as the minutes ticked by. Shouldn't there be some kind of sound out there? Anything?

"Why aren't they coming back in?" Jennifer whispered.

"I don't know," I said. I wondered if I should go out and check, but it had gotten dark while we were at Tom's, and I didn't want to be mistaken for the intruder.

We heard footsteps on the front porch, and my body stiffened. We all stared at the front door as it swung open. I breathed out when Alec and Thad walked through it.

"Hey," Thad said, and Sarah ran to him. "It's okay," he said, taking her in his arms.

I went to Alec, and he wrapped his arms around me. "What was it?" I asked.

"We didn't see anyone. We looked over the entire property, including the storage shed in the back. Whoever it was, they got out of here, and fast."

"I saw someone," Jennifer said, sounding defensive.

"We believe you," Alec assured her. "Did you get a look at them?"

Jennifer shook her head. "Not really. Sarah and I were getting ready to wrap presents in the bedroom, and I looked up and there was a face in the window. I screamed, and they left."

"Could you tell if it was a man or a woman?" he asked.

She shook her head again and went to sit in an armchair. "No. It happened so fast. I think they were wearing a hat or a hood. It was all so dark."

Alec looked at Sarah. "Sarah, did you see anything?"

She shook her head. "I had my back to the window. When Jennifer screamed, I turned to look, but whoever it was, they were gone."

"I'll give John a call and let him know," Alec said and went into a bedroom for privacy. I figured he was also letting him know about the missing dagger, and the others didn't need to know about that. There was no sense making them more scared than they already were.

"What were you two doing over at Tom's house?" Mama asked me.

"Putting that notebook back in his house," I said. "Mama, have you seen anyone over there this week? Like Tom's family? Or his daughter?" I asked.

She shook her head. "No, I thought it was odd that no one has been over there. I would have thought they would have wanted to go through his things and take mementos, or anything of any value. Seems like they would have to put the house up for sale at some point. I have to say, I don't look forward to new neighbors, though."

"That does seem odd that someone hasn't come to check on the house," I agreed. "Did Tom ever mention his daughter, Leslie, having a key? I know they weren't on speaking terms, but maybe she had one before they had a falling out?"

"No. She didn't have one. When she and Tom got into that fight a couple of years ago, he changed the locks," she said. "Why?"

"There was a vacuum over there the other day, and now it's gone," I said.

"Oh, that's probably Mabel Townsend. She cleaned Tom's home once a week. He felt sorry for her since her husband died about six years ago, and he paid her each week to clean. She probably took it home with her," Mama said.

I became alert when I heard the name Mabel Townsend. We hadn't mentioned the prescription bottle I had found at Tom's house to Mama.

"So she was there?" I asked. "Did you see her?"

"No, but I just figure that's what happened. She has a key, and it makes sense to me," she said, shrugging.

"Mom, what are we eating for dinner?" Thad asked, sitting down on the sofa and putting his feet on the coffee table. He had the remote in hand and didn't appear to be worried about the stranger in the window anymore.

"It depends on what you're going to make," I said. "You've been awfully lazy here lately, mister. You can't expect your grandmother to wait on you the whole time you're here."

"I'll make something," Sarah said, jumping up from her place beside him.

"Oh, that's so sweet of you, Sarah. Not like some other children I know," I said, looking pointedly at Thad.

"I can make chili dogs, mac and cheese, and spaghetti," Sarah said brightly.

"Oh," I said. "Well, maybe we'll go with spaghetti, and make a salad and garlic bread."

"Sounds good," she said and headed for the kitchen.

"Jennifer, Sarah could use some help," I said. I figured making dinner would help keep their minds off of the face in the window.

She looked up from her book and frowned. "I think I've been traumatized enough since I've been here, Mother. I need to rest."

"Come on Jennifer, give Sarah a hand," I encouraged.

She sighed and got to her feet, putting the book down on the coffee table.

Alec came back into the room and I realized we had run out of Tom's house so fast we hadn't locked the door.

"Alec, we need to go back and lock Tom's house up," I said. "We left in a hurry and I can't even remember if I closed the door behind me."

"Okay, I'll go do that. You can stay here," he said.

I followed him out the front door. "I'm coming with you."

"You never follow instructions," he said and took my hand.

"You know you love it though," I said, squeezing his hand. My banged up knee was really starting to feel the day's excitement, but I didn't mention it. He would insist I stay at the house and rest it if he knew.

"No, I really don't love it," he said.

"Mama said Mabel Townsend was Tom's housekeeper. That's the same name on that prescription medicine bottle we found," I said once we were out of earshot from the rest of the family. "She has a key."

"Really? I guess we need to put her on the list, then," he said.

The front door was standing open, and while that didn't surprise me, the hair on the back of my neck stood up. What if the intruder had ducked in there while Alec and Thad were searching my mother's property?

"Do you think the intruder is hiding in there?" I whispered.

"I doubt it, but you never know," he said, pushing the door wide open.

The living room light was still on, but the rest of the house was dark. Had we turned off the lights? We stepped into the living room and it was empty.

"Do you think it's okay?" I asked nervously.

"I think you should have stayed behind at your mother's house," he said.

"I'm going to stick with you," I said, and followed him closely as he walked down the dark hallway.

He reached up and flipped the hall light on, and I jumped reflexively.

He chuckled lightly. "Take it easy."

"Shouldn't you have your gun out?" I whispered. "You know, just in case?"

"Stop it," he said and flipped on the bedroom light. "See? Nothing here."

"Fine, but there are more rooms in this house," I pointed out as he opened the closet door.

"Nothing here, either."

We went from room to room, turning on all the lights, but the house was just as empty as it had been the first time we had entered it.

"There. Nothing here, nothing to be afraid of," he said when we had finished.

"Well, that's good news," I said. "Let's get back to the house and get something to eat. All this being scared business has made me work up an appetite. And I'm sure spaghetti will make my knee feel better."

"Oh, I'm sure," he agreed.

"It's a well-known fact that carbs make booboos heal faster. And tomorrow, why don't we drop in on Leslie Warren? Just to see how she's doing?" I suggested.

"I'd thought you'd never ask," he answered.

Chapter Twenty

LESLIE'S HOUSE LOOKED the same as when we were last here, except now the wreath that had been on the door was on the ground, to the side of the door. We had had a little wind the past couple of nights, but not enough to knock the wreath down.

I knocked on the door. I had brought her some white peppermint fudge and had carefully wrapped it up in a cute Christmas gift box with snowmen all over it. I could smell it through the box and wished I had brought extra to eat on the way over to her house.

"Maybe she isn't home," Alec said, taking a step back so he could see into her window without making it obvious.

I knocked again. "Persistence is key here."

After another minute, I heard movement in the house, then footsteps.

"See?" I asked him. The door slowly opened.

Leslie looked bad. She hadn't brushed her hair in a long while, and she had dark circles under her eyes. There was a stale odor that told me she also hadn't showered for several days. I smiled at her.

"Hi, Leslie. We were in the neighborhood and thought we'd stop by to check on you," I said brightly. "And I made you some white peppermint fudge." I held up the box so she could see it.

She stared at the box, trying to focus. I could smell alcohol, but I wasn't sure how fresh it was. Warily, her eyes went to mine. "Sorry, I haven't been feeling very well lately," she whispered. Her voice was hoarse, and she looked away.

"I'm sorry to hear that," I said sympathetically. "May we come in? We won't stay but a minute."

She looked at Alec, her eyes hooded from either grief or alcohol. I couldn't tell which.

"Hello, Leslie," Alec said softly. "We'd like to speak with you just for a moment."

"Okay," she said hesitantly, and took a couple of steps back, allowing the door to open further. "I'm afraid I haven't had a chance to clean up the place."

"Don't you worry yourself about it," I said, following her as she led the way to the living room.

She was right about not having a chance to clean up. There were newspaper pages scattered about the room, used paper plates, and empty Styrofoam soft drink cups. Three whiskey bottles sat on an end table, each one nearly empty. A very pregnant calico cat lay on one end of the sofa, and she picked it up and set it on the floor.

"Sorry for the mess," she said, not meeting my eyes.

"There's no reason to apologize," I said and sat down on the end of the sofa the cat had just vacated.

Alec sat on the overstuffed chair across from me. "Leslie, how have you been doing?" he asked.

"Oh, I guess about as well as I can be," she said, avoiding his gaze.

"We were just concerned about you," I said. It looked like she was really struggling since her father had died. "It's hard losing a loved one."

She let out a soft snort. "If you can call it that."

The box of fudge was still in my hand, and I considered putting it down on the coffee table, but something had spilled across most of the surface of the table, so I held onto it.

"Relationships can be difficult sometimes," I said softly. "But a parent never stops loving their child."

She looked up at me, her eyes blazing. "That might be true for a lot of people, but not for my father. I can tell you that much. He... he....," she said and trailed off.

I glanced at Alec, not sure if I was pushing too hard, and Alec was looking back at me.

"He what?" I encouraged, turning back to Leslie.

She looked down at her hands, and her face softened. "He was a good dad. When I was younger. I don't understand why that changed. Or maybe I do. Maybe when I started using the drugs, he was ashamed of me, and he just couldn't love me anymore." She looked up at me. "I never meant to get involved in drugs. It just... it just happened."

I reached a hand out and put it on hers. "A lot of people that try drugs end up addicted. And there are a lot of hard things we go through in life. There isn't a guidebook to tell us how to handle it when it's one of our loved ones."

"He should have loved me anyway," she pleaded with me. "Shouldn't he?"

I nodded. "I'm sure he did, he just might not have been able to express it," I said.

"Why did he leave my mother? I can see him leaving me, but her?" she asked.

The conversation was starting to make me feel anxious. She needed so many answers, and I was scrabbling to find them. She needed professional help, and all she had was me at that moment.

"Are you sure he did? Maybe he was still going to see her?" I asked, hoping she would tell more about that.

She sat back, and there was anger in her bloodshot eyes again. "No, he took her to that horrible place and dropped her off, and that was the end of it. Like she was some stray cat. He never went to see her again."

I looked at Alec for help.

"Leslie, we weren't around when all this happened. If what you say happened, then we believe you," he said and gave me a look.

I was surprised he was saying this after what Mama and Shelby had said. She obviously didn't remember things accurately because of the drugs.

"Well, it did happen!" Leslie insisted.

Alec nodded. "Okay. But we can't go back and change things. Now, what about getting you some help? You need to be able to look forward to the future and not back at the past. Maybe you can get some help with the drinking and drugs?"

She shook her head. "Oh, I don't do drugs no more. And that?" she said, indicating the whiskey bottles. "My boyfriend Stan was over, and he drank most of that. I hardly ever drink."

"Okay," Alec said. "What about some grief counseling? It can help tremendously to have someone guide you through this process."

She looked at him, considering. "I don't know about those kinds of things. Do you think it's a good idea?"

"I do. Before we leave to go back to Maine, we'll see if we can find a counselor someplace nearby and maybe get you set up with some therapy sessions," he said.

"That's a really good idea," I agreed. My man had a heart of gold.

She hesitated, but then said, "That would be really good." She suddenly looked a little brighter.

"Leslie, can I ask you, did you have a key to your father's house? Or were you over there at any time this week?" Alec asked.

"No. He asked me for the key back a couple of years ago. Said he didn't want me around," she said, her voice cracking. "Why?"

Alec shrugged. "Just wondering. It looked like someone might have been by there."

"Oh. Well, I didn't. My aunt and uncle might have. I haven't talked to them though. They don't like me either."

"Do you know of anyone else that might have had a key to your father's house?" I asked.

"Could have been almost anyone. He had lots of girlfriends. And there was a cleaning lady, I think. You know, Mabel Townsend? She was very rude as I recall, but I haven't spoken to her in years. She had the nerve to tell me my father wasn't my real father," she said, looking at the floor.

"Why would she say something like that?" I asked.

She shrugged. "She's just mean, I guess. But I knew it wasn't true. I look too much like my father." On the last part, her voice softened almost to a whisper.

It was true. Leslie looked too much like Tom to deny it. It was an odd thing for Mabel to say though.

I felt the phone in my pocket vibrate, and I resisted the urge to pull it out and look at it. It was probably one of the kids texting and asking what we were going to do today.

"Well, Leslie, we don't want to tie up any more of your time," Alec said. "We appreciate your taking the time to speak to us."

She looked up at him. "Oh, it's no trouble. I, well, I really wanted to say thank you. For helping me out at the funeral like y'all did that way." She looked away again, and color sprang to her cheeks.

"You're welcome," I said. "Sometimes people just need a little help through the hard spots in life."

She looked up at me. "I don't usually act that way. I guess I was just feeling out of sorts or somethin'."

"It's perfectly understandable. It was a stressful situation," I said and started digging through my purse. "I have a blog on grief. I don't update it much anymore, but there are a lot of articles there. It might help." I handed her a business card with the blog address on it.

"Thanks," she said, looking at the card.

I handed her the box of fudge, and we said our goodbyes as we walked to the front door. My heart went out to her. I didn't know if her boyfriend Stan existed or not, and if he did, I had to wonder if he was any help to her with her grief. He certainly hadn't shown up for the funeral when she needed him most. But we would find a counselor for her before we left, and maybe that would help. I felt my phone go off again, and this time it was someone calling, but I left it in my pocket. I didn't want to be rude.

Once inside the car, I asked, "Do you think she really believes her father abandoned her mother?"

"I think she does. And it isn't fair to her for anyone to try to force her to believe the truth," he said, starting the car. "That's something she has to come to on her own."

"No, I suppose not. Do you think she had anything to do with the missing dagger?"

He shrugged and pulled away from the curb. "It's hard to know for sure, but I don't think so. I think she's telling the truth about not having a key to Tom's house."

"Well, we need to find that counselor for her," I said. "I think it will help her a lot."

"We do. If we can, we'll find one that also handles drug and alcohol abuse. Maybe she'll decide during grief counseling that she needs help with that, as well."

As we pulled away, I couldn't help feeling as if we had let Leslie down, just like her father had. I hoped counseling would be what she needed to get her life back on track.

Then I remembered my phone. I pulled it out of my pocket and looked at it. There was a missed phone call from Thad as well as a text.

Mom, we can't find Jennifer. Call me.

"Oh no," I said. My heart pounded in my chest, and suddenly I couldn't breathe.

"What?" Alec asked.

"Jennifer's missing."

Chapter Twenty-One

ALEC SPED ALONG THE highway, headed back to my mother's house. Adrenaline coursed through my body, and all I could think of was that I wanted to jump out of the van and run for all I was worth.

I called Thad's cell phone, but there was no answer. I hung up and called Jennifer's, but no answer there, either. Last, I called Sarah.

"Hello!" she said in a rush. "Allie, Thad is out looking for Jennifer."

"Where is she? What happened?" I shouted, and then put the phone on speaker so Alec could hear.

"She walked down to the corner store. She said she'd be back in twenty minutes, but she's been gone for over three hours. Thad went to the store to look for her, but she wasn't there. I don't know if she went into the woods or not, but I don't think she would after we had that prowler," she said. "Where are you?"

"We're almost home. We'll be right there," I said.

"Don't worry, Sarah. She's probably found something interesting to do and lost track of time," Alec reassured her.

"Okay," Sarah said uncertainly.

"We'll see you in about three minutes, Sarah. I'm going to hang up," I said.

"Okay, bye," she said.

"It's okay, Allie. We're almost there," Alec said after I hung up. "Everything will be fine."

"I don't think she would go into the woods. She's afraid of her own shadow," I said.

"Call John. Tell him to get backup out here," he said. "I'm sure she's just lost track of time, though."

I called John's personal cell phone and relayed the information to him.

"We'll be right there," he said and hung up.

I bit my lower lip and prayed. Every bad thing I had ever seen in a movie danced across my mind as we drove. She had to be okay. She had just gone for a walk and would be home soon.

After what seemed like forever, we made it to Mama's house. She and Sarah stood out on the porch, waiting for us. I jumped from the van as soon as it stopped and ran to them.

"Have you heard anything?" I asked.

Mama shook her head. "Not a word. I don't know where Thad is now, either."

"All three of you search every inch of this property. Keep your phones on. I'm going into the woods. John and some backup will be here soon. Let them know what's going on," Alec said and sprinted out of the yard and toward the woods.

"Let's go," I told Mama and Sarah.

"We've already searched the house," Sarah said.

"I know, but humor me," I answered. We split up and went through all the rooms, calling for Jennifer. She wasn't a toddler, she was an adult, and yet, I wanted every inch of this property searched. A couple of minutes later, we met back in the living room.

"Okay, let's try outside," I said, trying not to break down. Every cell in my body said something bad had happened to my daughter. We headed to the storage shed, but it only contained a few boxes and an old abandoned bicycle. Mama didn't have a garage, only a carport, and we were out of places to look.

"We didn't look in the cellar," Mama said, looking at me wide-eyed.

"Let's go," I said, and we headed around to the back of the house. Mama's house was old, and the cellar was just that. A room under the house, that was only about half the size of the floor of the house. It had double wooden doors that opened from outside the house and wasn't accessible from inside.

I pulled open one door, and Sarah took hold of the other. The doors creaked on their hinges, and I peered into the darkness. Mama had stopped using the cellar nearly ten years earlier because of her hip, and spider webs covered part of the entrance.

"Jennifer?" I called.

There was no answer back. I picked up a nearby stick to beat down the spider webs and stepped down two concrete steps and called her name again. I tore down more spider webs with the stick and hesitated. The cellar had had no improvements since the house had been built and there wasn't a light switch near the entrance like more modern rooms would have. The only light in the room was a single bare hanging light bulb that turned on with a pull string. And it was in the middle of the room.

The sun was on the other side of the house and provided little light into the cellar. I went down three more steps into the darkness. "Jennifer? Please answer if you're down here," I said. The silence was the only answer.

"I'll go in," Mama said from behind me. "I'm used to it." I could hear a tremble in her voice.

"It's okay, I've got it," I said. "I'm sure she's not in here, anyway. There's no reason for her to be in here."

I hadn't mentioned the fact that one of Tom's daggers was missing. And I suddenly realized that it was dark the night Jennifer had seen a face in the window and Alec hadn't known about the cellar. I had forgotten all about it and thought Thad probably had too since he hadn't mentioned searching it. I heard sirens coming down the road, and it gave me some measure of comfort.

I took a deep breath and stepped down three more steps, stopping when I felt spider webs in my hair. I swung the stick madly into the air and forced myself to not scream. The cellar smelled damp and suffocating.

My knees trembled, and the bruised one ached. It's now or never, I thought. And I forced myself to take the rest of the steps down into the bottom of the cellar.

"You okay, Allie?" Sarah asked from above me.

"Yeah, I'm fine," I said. I swung the stick in front of myself and tried to remember how far into the room the string for the light was. It had been years since I had been down here. I could remember running down here to fetch canned peaches for Mama on hot summer evenings, and never feeling afraid. This was different.

I told myself I was not going to be afraid now. I forced myself to move forward, lightly swinging the stick until I hit something that felt different than a spider web, and I reached out for it, feeling the string. I held my breath and pulled the string, and the cellar was flooded with light. Thank goodness for a good quality light bulb.

I blinked in the light, looking around. There was an old folded up canvas tent that Jake and I had played with as kids, a couple of jars of ancient canned goods, and some boxes. Nothing more. I breathed out.

A mouse scampered out of the corner, and I screamed.

"Are you okay?" Mama called from up above.

"Allie, what's wrong?" Sarah cried.

I laughed. My nerves were on edge. "Nothing. Nothing at all. Just a mouse. I'm coming back up."

I turned the light out and headed back for the steps. Each step brought me blessedly closer to the sunlight.

"Okay, now what?" I asked at the top of the steps. I looked at my phone. Nothing.

Sarah called Thad, but there was no answer. "I don't know why he doesn't answer," she said. "He should answer."

"Sometimes the woods block the signal," I said. "He'll be okay."

I hoped it was true. I needed it to be true for both my kids and Alec.

We headed back to the front porch and waited. I've never been good at waiting, so I paced.

Chapter Twenty-Two

"WE'LL FIND HER," JOHN assured me.

"I know," I said, nodding and looking at my feet. I couldn't meet his eyes. I knew it was too soon to panic, but panic was welling up inside of me. Certainly she had just taken the long way back home. Or she'd taken a wrong turn. When she got home and saw all the sheriff's cars parked out in front of her grandmother's house, she'd laugh at us for being paranoid. That was the story I was telling myself.

"I'm going to go look for her again," he said and headed toward the woods.

Five deputies were combing the woods, along with Alec and Thad. All I wanted was for everyone to come home safe and sound.

Sarah's phone rang, and we all looked at it.

"Hello, Thad," she said. "Where are you?"

I jumped up from my place on the porch rail and stood beside her.

"Okay," she said.

I motioned for her phone.

"Your mom wants to talk to you."

I took the phone from her. "Thad, where are you? Did you find your sister?"

"I'm here in the woods. Alec found me, and we haven't seen Jennifer yet, but we will. Don't you worry about it," he said, sounding confident. I wanted to believe him. I really did. But my mind was running wild.

I sighed tiredly. "Okay. Just... find her."

"I will. Mom?" he asked.

"Yeah?"

"Alec told me about the dagger the night Jennifer saw the face in the window. But don't worry about it. It's going to be okay. I'll find her."

Tears sprang to my eyes, and it took all I had to keep from breaking down.

"I love you," I said.

"Love you, too. Bye."

I hung up and went into the house to get a glass of water and wipe my eyes. Everything was going to be fine. It had to be. There was no other choice in the matter. I chugged back a glass of water and then took a deep breath. My hand shook as I put the glass into the sink. Jennifer was just going for a walk. That's all. She'd be home, and we'd all laugh over the fuss we'd made.

My phone rang, and I looked at it. Alec.

"Hey," I said and waited.

"Hey. I just wanted to check in with you. I know waiting is hard. We haven't found her yet, but we will. I don't want you worrying. Everything will be fine."

"Okay," I whispered.

"Do you believe me?" he asked.

"Yes."

"Okay, I'll talk to you later."

I hung up the phone and headed back to the front porch. It was past noon now, and I wondered if this wait would ever end. It hadn't been long, but it still felt like forever.

"I'm going to take a look in the woods," I told Mama and Sarah.

"Now, Allie, maybe you should just stay put," Mama said.

"I can't just sit here any longer. I need to do something," I said, and bounded down the porch steps, wincing at the pain in my knee. Then I stopped and went back up the steps and went inside. Thad's pocketknife sat on the coffee table, and I picked it up and put it in my pocket, then headed back outside again. I half-limped, half-trotted into the woods, and then slowed to a fast walk, sticking with a trail that hadn't become completely overgrown with vegetation.

Thad's knife had a four-inch blade. I had no idea what I would do with it, but it made me feel better just having it in my pocket.

When I was further away from the house, I began to call Jennifer's name. Maybe she had twisted her ankle and was laying out here somewhere. It was cold out, and I hoped she was wearing a jacket. It would be awful if she had to spend the night out here in the woods. I didn't know if she would make it.

My knee was aching, but I forced myself to continue. Think about something else. Anything else, I told myself.

"Jennifer!" I called. I heard the crunching of leaves, and I stopped, my breathing came fast and heavy, and I tried to force myself to slow it down. I listened, trying to hear something else.

A squirrel scampered out from behind a tree, crunching leaves in its path, and I sighed. I needed to get myself together. I was letting my imagination run away with me.

"Please, Jennifer," I whispered.

Nothing.

"Jennifer!" I called out.

I took a deep breath and continued.

Thirty minutes passed, and I ran into Elmer.

"Anything?" I asked when I saw him.

He shook his head. "Nope. I doubt she's out here. I tell you, a girl like that probably found some boy to spend some time with."

Anger rose up inside of me. "A girl like what? Are you crazy? Jennifer wouldn't take off without telling someone."

He shrugged. "I'm just telling you, that's what usually happens in cases like this. She's out enjoying herself while everyone else is frantically searching for her. She's a pretty girl, you know."

I have never wanted to hit someone so much in my entire life. My hands balled into fists, and I closed my eyes for a second. When I opened them, I was more in control. A little. "I have a daughter to search for," I said and kept heading down the trail.

"Hey, it's not safe for you to be in these woods alone," he said.

I ignored him. If I had to talk to him anymore, I would say something I would regret.

As the afternoon wore on, my knee swelled more, and my jeans became tight around my leg. Walking on it was getting harder, and I was getting deeper and deeper into the woods. I stopped and called for her again. "Jennifer! Jennifer!"

The silence nearly made me break down. I turned around and headed back, limping the whole way. I was afraid I would have to stop and wouldn't be able to walk out of the woods. Then I would need my own rescue party. Tears streamed down my face, and I let them fall. No one could see me here. I wanted to call Alec or Thad, but I already knew what the answer to my unspoken question was. It was pointless.

It was late afternoon when I left the edge of the woods. The porch was empty, and I knew Mama and Sarah had gone inside. My knee was screaming at me, and all I wanted was some ibuprofen to take the pain away. I hobbled the rest of the way to the house and up the steps.

I could smell chicken frying in the kitchen, and I pushed the door open.

Mama and Sarah spun around to look at me.

"Anything?" Mama asked.

I shook my head and headed to the sink for some water.

"We decided to make chicken and biscuits for everyone. I'm sure they've all got to be starving by now," Mama said.

"That's a good idea," I said between gulps of water. I limped over to the cupboard that Mama kept medicine in and got the ibuprofen.

"Your knee must be hurting really bad," Sarah said, as she rolled the biscuits out.

I nodded and took three pills and drank the rest of the glass of water. I hobbled over to the table and sat down, groaning a little as my knee bent. I was going to have to cut my jeans off my leg tonight.

"We haven't heard anything back from anyone," Sarah said quietly.

"I know," I said.

Chapter Twenty-Three

I HADN'T HAD ANYTHING to eat since breakfast, and when Mama sat a plate with two biscuits in front of me, my stomach growled. She had put butter and strawberry jam on them and set a glass of milk beside the plate. I devoured the biscuits and chugged the glass of milk, and felt a renewed surge of energy. I hadn't realized how hungry I was.

Mama put a hand on my shoulder. "They'll find her."

I nodded.

"I called Shelby and Jake. They're on their way down here to help."

I nodded again.

Mama went over and opened her junk drawer and pulled out a twist tie. I jumped up, hobbled over, and pulled the drawer open as she was closing it. I fished out the key to Tom's house.

"Where are you going?" Mama asked as I headed out the door.

I didn't answer her. I was on a mission. The ibuprofen hadn't had a chance to kick in yet, but I felt better after having had something to eat. Tom's house was dark. I turned the key in the lock and pushed it open.

The stillness made me shiver. We had left all the blinds in the house closed in case the locals decided to get nosey and check out a murder victim's house. I flipped on the light in the living room and entered the room, closing the door behind me. My first urge was to call for Jennifer, but something told me not to.

I limped across the room, trying to keep from making noise as I favored my hurt knee. I headed to the kitchen and turned the light on. The plant was sitting on the countertop, and I went to it and put it into the sink, and turned the water to a slow stream. I really needed to take it back to Mama. I shut the water off and turned around. The kitchen looked the same.

I headed out of the kitchen, flipping the light off as I left. As I hobbled through the living room again, something made me stop. I looked around. What was it?

Then I saw it. The vacuum was sitting in the same place by the wall where it had been the first time we were there. My heart leaped in my chest. I looked down at the carpet, and there seemed to be fresh vacuum marks. Was I imagining it?

I tried to steady my breathing. My first instinct was to run, but I couldn't as long as I didn't know whether Jennifer was in here or not. I pulled my phone out of my pocket and texted Alec.

Just an FYI. I'm in Tom's house, and the vacuum is back. Everything's ok. I'm just letting you know where I am.

I put my phone on mute and stuck it back in my pocket. I moved as quietly as I could and headed down the hall. The door creaked as I opened Tom's bedroom door. I flipped the light on, and it was empty. I let my breath out and hobbled over to the closet and opened it quickly before I had enough time to allow fear to build up. Empty.

I turned around and headed back down the hallway. I was being silly. Nothing was going on here. Except for the vacuum. Something was going on with that vacuum.

The door to the guest bedroom was open a crack, and I tried to remember if we had left it that way. My heart pounded as I pushed it open and turned the light on. My eyes blinked, unsure if what I was seeing was real or not. *It was.*

"Jennifer!" I cried and ran to the bed.

Her hands were tied in front of her, and her eyes were closed. She wasn't moving.

"Oh, Jennifer," I said, reaching for her bound hands.

The bedroom door slammed behind me, and I whirled around just in time to see a woman with short, dark curly hair bring a brick down on my head.

Chapter Twenty-Four

I WOKE UP IN A DARK place. My head screamed at me as I fought for consciousness. I tried to remember what had happened when I felt something moving beside me. It felt like I was lying on a bed, but the room was pitch black, and I couldn't make anything out. *Where was I?*

I tried to speak, making a 'J' sound, but couldn't get the word out. What was wrong with me?

"Mom?" Jennifer said weakly from beside me.

"Jen," I forced out of my dry mouth.

"Mom, what's happening?" she asked. I could hear the fear in her voice, and I hoped she wasn't hurt.

"I don't know," I said. "Are you hurt?"

"I don't think so. She made me drink something, and it made me sleep. My hands are tied."

I strained at the bonds on my own wrists, not sure what was holding me. The light suddenly went on, and the woman was standing near the door, staring at us. I wanted to scream, but I was too terrified and couldn't find my voice.

"I don't know why you had to do it," the woman said. She stared glassy-eyed at us.

I tried to open my mouth, but it felt like it was glued shut. I licked my lips and tried again. "Do what?" I croaked.

"You killed Tom," she said, her eyes getting wider.

I shook my head. "No, I didn't," I said.

"She did!" she said, pointing at Jennifer.

Jennifer whimpered and pushed her head up against my back.

"No, she found him. He was already dead," I said. That was when I noticed the dagger with blue crystals on the handle. She held it by her side, close to her body. I swallowed hard.

"I know the truth," the woman said, nodding slowly.

I remembered Mama had said the cleaning woman's name was Mabel. "Mabel, we would never hurt Tom. Tom was our friend. We want to find the person that did this. We want to help you find them."

I could see the hesitation in her face. "You can do that?"

I nodded. "Yes. I can help you. But you need to untie me so I can help."

She shook her head. "No, it's a trap. You're lying to me."

"No, I swear. I wouldn't lie to you. I want to find the person that killed Tom."

My head throbbed, and I felt nauseous. The bright light in the bedroom made it worse, and the room started to spin. What was she going to do to us? If I could just get her to untie me, we would have a chance.

"Please. I really do want to help you," I said. "We need to work together to figure this out."

She narrowed her eyes at me. "Don't try to confuse me," she said.

She looked to be in her late sixties, but she was stout. On a good day, I knew I could take her. But in my current condition, I wasn't sure. My eyes rolled back as a wave of pain surged through my head.

The door suddenly burst open, and Alec knocked Mabel to the floor. She screamed, and the dagger flew from her hand. She raised a hand to strike Alec, but he grabbed her arm.

"Let me go!" she screamed.

"What's happening?" Jennifer cried from behind me. Her face was still buried in my back, and I knew she was too scared to look.

"Alec is here."

Alec wrestled with Mabel on the floor, then he flipped her over and held her down. She lay beneath him, sobbing.

"They killed my husband! They killed Tom!" she cried.

Alec and I looked at each other wide-eyed. *Husband?*

"Mom! Jennifer!" Thad cried, stepping around Alec and Mabel, barely glancing at them. He rushed to the bedside and reached for his pocketknife.

"It's in my pocket, underneath me," I said.

He reached for the dagger on the floor instead, and cut away what held me, then worked on Jennifer's bonds. I slowly brought my arms around and rubbed my wrists. Blood rushed to the parts of my body that had been cramping up. I looked, and she had tied me with one of Tom's ties.

"Are you both okay?" Thad asked. I could see the fear in his eyes.

"I'm okay. Jen?"

She nodded. "Yeah."

Alec was on the phone, calling John for backup, and I forced myself to sit up. Pain flooded my head with the effort, and I squinted my eyes shut.

"You're bleeding," Thad said and left the room. He was back in a few seconds with a wet washcloth, and he dabbed at the side of my head.

I pulled away in pain and saw the blood on the white washcloth. Everything started to go black. I breathed in deeply to keep from fainting.

"We need an ambulance," Thad said to Alec.

"No, we don't. I'm okay. Just have a heck of a headache is all," I said, holding the side of my head. I took the washcloth from Thad and dabbed at my head again.

"Jennifer, do you need an ambulance?" Alec asked.

She shook her head, staring at the floor. "I'm okay."

"I want you checked out," he said to me and called for an ambulance anyway.

Mabel lay on the floor and whimpered, and I lay back on the bed. All I wanted was something to make the headache go away, and to sleep.

Chapter Twenty-Five

CHRISTMAS MORNING WE gathered around the Christmas tree, opening presents. My head still ached off and on throughout the night and into the morning, but it was getting better. As I looked around the room at my family, my eyes filled with tears. This could have been a completely different Christmas morning if Alec and Thad hadn't shown up when they did.

I took a sip of my hot cocoa and leaned my head against Alec's shoulder. The smell of baking cinnamon rolls filled the house, courtesy of Jennifer and Sarah. I took a deep breath and savored the moment. We had been through a lot, but we were all in one piece. I was a banged-up piece, but it was still one piece.

When the cinnamon rolls were done, Sarah jumped up and took them out of the oven, cut them, and put them on plates. Jennifer handed the plates out, and we ate in the living room, watching the lights twinkling on the Christmas tree.

Alec had gotten home late last night after having gone down with John to process Mabel.

"Why did Mabel kill Tom?" I asked Alec as everyone settled down to eat cinnamon rolls.

"Well, it seems she thought they had a relationship. She had been cleaning his house for a few years, and she wanted to date him, but he wasn't interested. So she pretended to be his wife. When she told him she was moving in, he told her he didn't want that. She persisted, insisting they were married, and he told her he didn't want her cleaning his house anymore," he said.

"She pretended to be his wife?" I asked. "And Tom was aware she was pretending? I mean, before she told him she was moving in?"

He shrugged. "I have the feeling it was something she wanted so badly, but she didn't say it out loud until she told him she was moving in. Tom was probably shocked, and refused."

"Wow," Jennifer said.

"Wow is right," I said.

"But did she realize she was making all of this up? Now that she's been arrested?" Thad asked.

He nodded. "She admitted that she had taken things too far, but she seemed to have difficulty with reality. For the record, John thinks its all an act."

"Seriously?" I asked.

He nodded. "I didn't believe it at first, but the more we talked to her, the more I had to agree. She's pretending to be confused about what happened."

"She kept saying that I killed him," Jennifer said. "Why would she think that?"

"She said she had seen you do it. What we think really happened was that she killed him in a fit of passion, and then hid when she saw you bringing him the chicken and dumplings.

We think that's when she decided to blame you if she ever got caught," he explained.

"I didn't kill him," Jennifer said, shaking her head.

Alec smiled. "We know that. You didn't have enough time. We're all a witness to that."

"Why did she ditch the murder weapon in the woods?" Thad asked.

Alec shrugged. "I'm not really sure. She may have been in a panic and ran out there, and either dropped it or tried to hide it in the woods. Every time we brought up the fact that Tom was stabbed to death, she would go into a panic and start screaming and crying hysterically."

"Wow," I said. "Why did she come back and grab Jennifer?"

"She thought Jennifer saw more than she had. That's why she followed her around the Christmas carnival and spied on her here at the house."

"Ah," I said, nodding my head. "The telltale heart. The guilt was eating her alive."

"That's a shame," Mama said, looking down at her hands. "I always thought Mabel was a little odd, but I never thought she was capable of killing someone."

I chuckled. "It's hard to know about some people," I said, shaking my head.

"She brought him those gingerbread cookies in an attempt to persuade Tom to allow her to move in. When he refused again, she got angry and stabbed him with the dagger she had stolen from his collection," Alec said.

"So sad," Mama murmured.

I took a bite of my cinnamon roll. It was just as good as mine, and I was proud of the girls. I had been worried about Sarah fitting into the family, but this trip made me change my mind. She cared about Thad, and that was enough for me.

I finished my cinnamon roll, and then got up and limped into the kitchen and put my plate in the sink. It would be good to get home. I needed the rest. I had never expected Christmas to be scary, but that's what it had been. I just wanted to sleep in my own bed and forget this ever happened.

Alec and I had new careers to begin in January. Careers we had yet to iron out the details on, but we had time.

THE END

Sneak Peek

Ice Cold Murder

A Freshly Baked Cozy Mystery, book 5

Chapter One

It had never felt so good to be home. I had enjoyed spending Christmas with my mother in my hometown of Goose Bay, Alabama, but my daughter Jennifer and I had come too close to becoming murder victims. Now that a new year was here, I had made up my mind that it was going to be a good one. I had a new love in my life, and I was working on a new career, even if I hadn't pinned down all the details yet.

The sun was shining down on Alec and me as we ran through my neighborhood. In spite of the early morning cold, I could tell it was going to be a warm day. Warm for January in Maine, at least.

I took a swig from my water bottle, and we crossed the street and headed for my house. The closer we got to the marathon we planned to run in May, the less prepared I felt. I still had an extra five pounds I needed to lose after spending Christmas with my mother. Darn those fresh buttermilk biscuits slathered in butter and homemade strawberry jam. But a girl has gotta do what a girl has gotta do, and now I was paying the price.

"I have the best idea ever," Alec said, as we finished our run and headed inside my house.

"Do tell," I said and took a seat on the bench located along a wall inside my mudroom. I grabbed my everyday shoes from under the bench and began untying my running shoes. After a few weeks of treadmill running and staring at a blank wall, I had paid extra for a pair of shoes that would help stay me on my feet on icy and snowy roads and sidewalks. I had missed running outside.

"Let's make snow cream," he said. "I haven't made it in a couple of years."

"Snow cream? Thaddeus used to make that. But it's sunny out, and the weather channel said there wouldn't be any new snow for a couple of days," I pointed out. Thaddeus was my late husband, and he had loved the outdoors.

He shrugged. "So? It snowed last night."

He was right. It *had* snowed the previous evening, but we hadn't thought ahead to put a bowl out to catch clean snow. "We missed the snow," I said. "We can watch and put a bowl out when it gets ready to snow again."

"Why?" he asked. He had his right foot on the bench, tying his shoe.

"Because we want clean snow? If we're going to eat it, right?" I wasn't sure why he wasn't making the connection.

He chuckled. "We'll get clean snow. We're going to drive out to the woods and find some fresh, clean snow. We'll fill up a bucket and make a big bowl of snow cream."

"Uh, wait a minute," I said. "You're going to get the snow off the ground? And eat it?" He had to be out of his mind. Who did that? I wanted my snow to be guaranteed clean, without any critters having made tracks, or worse, through it.

"That's right, smarty pants. Right off the ground. It tastes better that way. Back to nature and all that."

"Says you. What if Yogi Bear, you know, did his business in it?" I asked, raising an eyebrow at him. Surely he had thought of that, right?

He laughed and put his foot back on the floor. "I'm pretty sure we'll be able to tell if Yogi has been anywhere near the snow we're going to get. I promise you, we'll get clean snow. I've been doing this all my life, and I know what I'm doing."

I sighed. "Well, I guess if you know what you're doing. But let's get some breakfast first. I'm starving."

I wasn't at all sure he knew what he was talking about. Everyone I knew that went to the trouble of making snow cream simply left a large bowl or bucket outside when it was snowing and collected what they needed. Sure, I'd heard of people going out to the woods to get snow, but I figured all those people must be doomsday preppers or whatever it was they were calling themselves these days.

I quickly scrambled up some eggs, and Alec made toast and coffee. Nothing fancy, but it was warm and filling. There was something about the smell of coffee on a winter morning that made me happy. It also made me feel warm and cozy, and I wondered if it was too early in the morning for a nap. I had flannel sheets on my bed, and the long run had worn me out. A nap sounded good.

"Hey," Jennifer said sleepily as she wandered into the kitchen and stretched. She wore flannel pajamas and white fluffy bunny slippers. Her tattered Hello Kitty bathrobe was wrapped loosely around her body.

"Good morning, Jennifer," Alec said. His dark hair was mussed after our run, but he was still handsome as ever.

Jennifer hadn't been crazy when Alec first made an appearance in our lives, but ever since our we-almost-got-murdered scare last month, she had been nicer to Alec. I didn't raise any fool. She knew Alec had a gun and that he knew how to use it. That sort of thing could come in handy in an emergency, and it had when a crazed murderer had taken both of us hostage.

"There are more scrambled eggs in the skillet, but you'll have to make your own toast," I said.

"And guess what we're doing?" Alec asked her, sounding like a kid on Christmas morning.

"What?" she asked, stumbling to the coffee maker and pouring herself a cup.

"We're going out to the woods to collect some snow and make snow cream," he said happily.

She turned and looked at him with an arched brow. "Why are you going out to the woods?"

"He likes his snow wild-caught. It has a different bouquet than domesticated snow," I supplied.

"Yeah, I bet it has a different bouquet. Eau de deer pee," she said.

I snickered. Like mother, like daughter.

Alec sighed. "You two are not very adventurous. You need to step out of your comfort zones. I assure you, other people make snow cream this way and live to tell the tale."

"Yes, people who live in tents and don't have access to electricity," I said.

Alec gave me the stink eye, and I smiled big at him. We finished up our breakfast and got ready to leave.

"You sure you don't want to come along, Jennifer?" Alec asked as we headed out the door.

"Nope. I'm good. Thanks," she said, slumping over her cup of coffee at the kitchen table, phone in hand. Jennifer had never been a morning person.

Alec's black SUV had belonged to the police department, and when he retired on December 31st, it had gone back. He was on foot until he could find a car he liked. I let him drive my car since he was sure he knew exactly where to get clean snow. We left town behind us, and after fifteen minutes of driving out into nowhere, I was starting to get worried. Just where was this clean snow?

"Hey, where are we going?" I finally asked him. "We've been driving a long time."

He smiled. "You're such a worrywart," he said and pulled off the road. "We'll walk into the woods a little way, and there will be miles and miles of clean snow."

"Okay, if you're sure about that," I mumbled and got out of the car, pulling my coat closer. A breeze had kicked up, and I wondered if I was wrong about it being a warm day or if the weather was just somehow colder out in the wild.

Alec reached into the backseat of my car and pulled out the two white buckets and two small shovels we had brought. The buckets had originally held ice cream and were two and a half gallons each. I wondered if we needed that much snow. It seemed like overkill.

"Come on," he said, taking my gloved hand.

The snow along the side of the road had been plowed, and the area was smooth, but as we got closer to the edge of the woods, I realized I'd made a mistake in not putting boots on. My feet were already wet and cold, and we hadn't even walked through deep snow yet.

"I'm not wearing appropriate shoes for this," I said.

"I know, but it will only take us a few minutes. I promise," he said. "We'll turn the heater on high on the way back."

We walked into the woods, and the snow was surprisingly still light and fluffy. I looked at it, wondering how many animals had tread through it, but I didn't see any obvious signs. Maybe Alec did know what he was talking about.

"How much further?" I asked, as my breath left my mouth in puffs of white clouds.

"Just over here, I think," he said. "We want to try and scoop up the top layer as much as possible, otherwise our snow cream will be filled with hard ice."

"Okay," I said. "What about over there?" I saw a mound of snow, and it looked pristine. I was sure no animal had gone anywhere near it.

"That looks good. You start over there, and I'll start right over here," he said, indicating a smaller mound on his left.

"Are we going to fill up both buckets?" I asked, heading to the larger mound I had spotted.

"Yeah, mound them up, too. Some of it will melt on the way home. We can put the buckets in the trunk so it'll stay colder."

I stopped in front of the mound and examined it, then walked slowly around it. I bent over and stuck my finger in it. It looked clean beneath the surface. I stood up straight and appraised it. It looked as clean as could be, and I decided it would pass muster.

Using my small shovel, I scooped up a layer of snow and put it in the bucket. I scooped a second time and hit something solid. *That's odd*. I tried another spot and scooped some off the top and put it in the bucket, and then tried again in another place and hit something hard again. I tried a few more spots and kept hitting something solid after the first scoop. I glanced over at Alec who seemed to be scooping away at the light, fluffy snow and getting his bucket filled nicely. *Huh. This might be harder than I thought.*

Buy Ice Cold Murder on Amazon

https://www.amazon.com/
Ice-Cold-Murder-Freshly-Mystery-ebook/dp/B01MU16R11

If you'd like updates on the newest books I'm writing, follow me on Amazon and Facebook:

https://www.facebook.com/
Kathleen-Suzette-Kate-Bell-authors-759206390932120/

https://www.amazon.com/Kathleen-Suzette/e/
B07B7D2S4W/ref=dp_byline_cont_pop_ebooks_1

Made in the USA
Monee, IL
01 September 2021

76812134R00104